A SARAH DOUCETTE JEAN-LOUIS MYSTERY

SECRETS, SPELLS ← AND → SNAKE EYES

PART DEUX

MYRA JOLIVET

Pushed Times Publishing

SECRETS, SPELLS AND SNAKE EYES

A Sarah Doucette Jean-Louis Mystery, Part Deux

Myra Jolivet

This book is a work of fiction. All of the characters, organizations and events portrayed in this novel are either products of the author's imagination or are used fictitiously.

http://myrawritesback.blogspot.com

ISBN: 099080321X
ISBN 13: 9780990803218

Cover design by: Mark Gelotte, The Art of Books

"Lache pas la patate."
Don't drop the potato!

This is a Creole expression used when hunters would toss hot potatoes that had been cooked over a campfire to each other. The expression came to mean, "Hang in there!"

Acknowledgments

To the people who encourage me to keep telling stories and to everyone who reads them.

Prologue

I never thought that a hand could look wicked, but the gloved hand that slammed the door of a medicine cabinet so hard it bounced back open, clearly had an evil intention. The sounds were crisp and clear. I could hear muffled screams and desperate wrestling. Someone, a man, struggled to hold onto his life while gloved hands covered his mouth and neck. The man tried to fight the hands, but he couldn't. The violent movement was part of a short, bitter vision that crept into my deep sleep and woke me up with a sour stomach and sweat-drenched fear.

It didn't make sense for me to walk around the house as if on patrol, but I did. My visions played as mind movies into the future, controlling my emotions and stoking my fears. My hands shook as I looked into my medicine cabinet and checked the locks on my door.

I've got to find out how to control these damn visions. I want them to work for me rather than me frantically trying to figure them out. They terrify me.

Whether in a dream state or trance, my psychic intuitive visions invaded my mind space without my command. Each time they appeared with brain-numbing pain and nausea, a foul tasting mystery of code I had to learn to decipher in order to help myself and others.

I looked around my bedroom for signs of moved furniture or an intruder, but there was only a faint stream of light from the street, angling between my planter's shades, which created a pointed dart on the wood floor. The rest of the room was moonless, with the eerie peace of my spirit life. *Mo pa komprann. I don't understand. I used my limited Creole French in frustration.*

I wanted to hear my late Aunt Cat's voice in her thick Creole accent saying, "Just hang in dere cher, lache pas la patate. Da gift will always lead you to what you need to know. You will understand, cher. You will komprann." Aunt Cat's name was Catin, pronounced with a soft 'an' at the end which is common of 'in' endings in French. She was my spiritual mentor and guide. Before her death, she schooled me in the gift of visions and how they can be used to heal, to expose, to inspire and to exact justice. But unfortunately, before she passed on, I didn't learn how to control them. I was the only one of my generation with the gift and sometimes it felt like a curse.

I hope you're right, Auntie. I need to understand a lot more than I do.

I wanted the strong comfort of Aunt Cat. All I had now was the sensation of her voice from the spirit world. It came to me clearly and I appreciated that, but I missed her petite presence. Aunt Cat was a honey-colored, older version of my mother with high cheek bones, a straight nose and barely-there lips. Her baby fine hair was wavy and though gray, never lost its shine. Ironically, I was a student of mind sciences. But my second sight defied all science, even the wisdom of Carl Jung, whose philosophies I had modeled as a family therapist. For the eerie pictures from another world to land in my head was a frightful comedy. But after a year of loss of a fiancé and nearly my life, I was ready to use these damn gifts, like a master, and to find out where and why hands in black gloves were killing a young man.

By now, I had accepted the fact that my gift of visions was not to be ignored. The visions presented themselves as new chapters, opening the path to another life journey. I just hoped that this time I could avoid the threat of death.

CHAPTER ONE

When I was two years old, I ate a cigarette butt and threw it up. I had raided the ashtrays after a party my parents hosted. My adult life played out that same way—want, acquire, and then purge. I was a strange kid who would go on to live a scary-book life. I had learned what to want and how to acquire it, and then life would take me on a cleansing purge. A new psychic vision put the taste of that cigarette butt in my mouth.

I liked the theme song of the Wicked Witch of the West from *The Wizard of Oz*. Those days I used it as my mobile phone ring tone. It broke into my meditative Sunday morning at home in Oakland's Lake Merritt area. I had filled my condo with the sweet smells of lavender candles and incense, Gregorian chants, and the repeating sound of water in my living room fountain. I had a lot of time to meditate. My family-therapy practice had cratered under the afterglow of public scandal, and I wasn't sure what I really wanted to do.

I answered the phone and hid my irritation. "Hello?"

"Sarah? It's Manuel."

Manuel was the only thing I was sure that at some point, I really wanted to do. His voice caused the backs of my knees to tingle. Although no longer attorney and client, we had continued to keep our chemistry to harmless flirting.

"Hi, Manuel."

"How was the reunion in Louisiana?" he asked.

"Pretty good." I was stuck in nervous, two-word answers.

"Sarah, like I told you before you left for Louisiana, I want you to work some cases for me. Little did I know I'd have one helluva case by the time you got back. Are you game, or are you planning to reopen your family therapy practice?" Manuel asked.

"Ha. What practice? I'm still the psychic freak whose patients left when she was outed as the mistress at the center of the area's biggest murder scandal. Remember?" I giggled.

"Oh, good. You're available," Manuel joked.

"Still sensitive, I see."

Manuel's humor was sarcastic and delicious. But his voice quickly turned serious. I could tell that this case was personal.

"I need to meet with you to give you more details about this one. But here's the gist: My colleague's son is being framed for a murder I'm sure he didn't commit. Sarah, I gotta help this kid. He has a history of drugs, but he's been clean for a year. This situation is so fucked up that I'm not sure where to start. I have great respect for your ability to see beyond the facts. I need that and all of your skills to help my investigator. There's a complexity to this case that I don't think he'll get." There was an undertone of sadness in Manuel's voice.

"Manuel...I'm not sure how or if I can help, but you know I'll try," I said.

"Well, can you meet me for dinner? I want to fill you in on what we know so far," he requested.

"Of course."

"Meet me at Tony's Beach Restaurant tonight in the city. I'll have a quiet table at seven. And, Sarah, thank you. This kid is worth it, and I do believe you can make the difference for him."

"Sure. See you at seven." I hung up.

I released my legs from the lotus position, and as I stood up, my head swirled. Colors flashed between my temples, and nausea pierced the back of my tongue. It was a sign one of my now infamous visions was making an appearance. I watched images in black and white stream through my mind. Evil, soulless snake eyes seemed to stare straight into mine. They disappeared. I refused to let the chill climbing up my back disrupt my excitement in preparing to have dinner with Manuel and quality time in my closet. My custom closet was the envy of all friends and haters. My clothes collection nurtured my ego.

I wanted Manuel to remember I had a kickin' body riding under my intuitive, five-dimensional mind, so I went for clingy with taste and quickly laid out a purple-and-red long-sleeved silk dress; black, red-bottomed shoes; and gold jewelry.

This particular Sunday afternoon was reserved for my girls, Nikeba and Sandy. These martini-laced lunches were my therapy. The three of us met decades earlier at Berkeley High. They had become the family my blood siblings were not. My family held tightly to our old-world Louisiana Creole culture. It was Stepford robotic conformity long before *The Stepford Wives* was a movie. Our culture held little tolerance for individuality; women had husbands before age twenty-five, period. Mothers had the power to choose your escort for your debutante cotillion or your husband, even if you didn't like either of them. I had blown that marriage requirement by decades. I had come to realize that family pressures and disappointments in a forty-plus single me had caused me to make some of my worst relationship decisions. Nikeba and Sandy were my oasis from the judgers. Although we at times had bitter arguments and differing opinions, we remained committed friends with the love of sisters. We'd met in high-school gym class and decided to stay in touch during our college years. Within the accepted time frame, they met and married wonderful husbands, whereas I provided bad dating comic relief.

"I told Steve that I want a real vacation this year. None of this Napa shit; I want an airplane involved. We work, work, and cheat ourselves when it's time to play." Nikeba was firm but not angry. She and her husband seemed to never express bitter anger. I hadn't witnessed harsh words between them in more than twenty years. Nikeba was a striking woman. Her average height was framed in chocolate velvet skin and a dark brown, short afro hairdo. She had a long, lean face and despite being of different races, she and her Jewish husband resembled each other. Steve Newman's narrow face anchored salt and pepper gray hair and alarming hazel eyes. He had the look of a Berkeley professor on non-courtroom days with blazers and khaki pants, but like Nikeba, he was all attorney. Her wardrobe choices were not on my radar. Nikeba's outfits ranged from African-inspired prints and caftans, to buttoned-up black or navy suits with white shirts on her lawyering days. The subject of time off had come up as Sandy spread out images of blue sky, a flawless beach, and laughter—her photos from Cabo, taken during their family vacation. Sandy was a 5-foot-11 redhead. Her curly hair had the look of singer Carole King and the refinement of a $200 cut. Sandy preferred casual clothes and wore yoga pants even when not headed to a class. Her Marin County upbringing revealed itself in understated refinement. She seldom wore jewelry or anything shiny. She loved pastel shirts and solid colored, stretchy pants with ballet flats or running shoes. She had left corporate America to be a stay-at-home mom to their daughter once her husband's business as a general contractor took off. Raphael Acosta was from East L.A. and the East Bay. His Chicano heritage gifted him with beautiful brown skin, dark wavy hair and dreamy dark eyes. Raphael had an athletic build which attracted the stares of women whenever he entered a room. Most days he dressed like the head of a construction company with jeans and expensive shirts rolled up at the sleeves.

My mind drifted as I looked at their pictures. A beautiful engagement party and dreams of a honeymoon and family life were less than a year ago. My engagement to Michael had ended tragically. I had come so close to living my dream, only to land back in the seat of the fifth wheel.

"Sarah? Sarah!" Nikeba raised her voice. A few of the diners of Sea-Son's Restaurant in Jack London Square glared at her.

My attention rejoined the table.

"Oh. What?" I asked.

"Steve's prison contacts say that Michael's been asking about you."

"Really? Why?" I asked.

"Hell if I know. I told Steve you wouldn't care." A vodka-rinsed Nikeba shook her head yes but meant no.

"I wonder what he wants," Sandy whispered, leaning into the table— as if anyone knew that we were the stars of last year's local scandal.

The patio seats at Sea-Son's were perfect for staring into the water of the Oakland/Alameda estuary to San Francisco Bay. Nikeba and Sandy's debate of whether I should visit Michael at the prison moved into a distant background. I wasn't sure if I was inspired by the Kettle One and Castelvetrano olives or nursing a mild depression, but I stared backward into time, thinking of buying my wedding gown and invitations. I smiled, as I remembered giggling with Ma-ma like children at the cake tasting. And I felt the knife-sharp pain of learning the truth about Michael. I squeezed one year into a few seconds, and my heart sank into the memories.

"You know?" Sandy asked.

"What?" I asked.

"Sarah, you're not yourself. You barely touched your drink and you're not in the conversation. What's up?" Nikeba steadied her tipsy gaze blinking her eyes.

"Yeah. Is something wrong?" Sandy asked.

"No, well, yes. I was thinking about last year, Michael, you know." I answered.

Nikeba and Sandy both looked down at their drinks. "Put it behind you, girl. And you don't need to visit or hear anymore about Michael. I'm sorry I told you about him." Nikeba encouraged.

"Yeah, let it stay in the past." Sandy patted my arm.

"I will, eventually. And Nikeba don't keep information about Michael away from me. In some weird way, it helps." I insisted.

"Ok. If you want me to. He's been asking for you like some maniac. Oh yeah, he is a maniac." We all laughed.

"From the moving on department, I didn't tell you guys, but I have dinner with Manuel tonight, so I need to leave early." I managed to focus.

"Oohhhhhh, ahhhhhh, Manuel," Sandy sang.

"Silly. It's business." I wrestled with my mouth to hide a smile.

"Business? What kind of business?" Nikeba asked.

"He thinks I can help with some cases and we're meeting for dinner to talk about the first one," I reluctantly shared.

Nikeba was a hard core attorney. She and her husband, had known Manuel for years when they recommended he represent me during last year's murder trial. I didn't want to hear her warnings about spending too much time with Manuel. She surprised me.

"Good idea, Sarah. I think you need something to dig into," she said.

"I really do. I've been bored and spending a lot more time with Ma-ma, so you know it's time for me to do something." I laughed.

"Whew. You definitely need a project." Nikeba whistled.

"He is gorgeous, too!" Sandy's comment was a bit too loud and a little random.

We laughed.

"Yeah. He is fine. But he's a player. That's all I'll say." Nikeba held back, uncharacteristically. She was tipsy and motioned awkwardly to the waiter. "Can we get three coffees?"

He nodded.

"Who said we wanted coffees?" Sandy argued, playfully.

"Drink coffee, you lightweight. I don't want Steve to have to get both of us out of jail today," Nikeba insisted.

"Well, no coffee for me, I didn't drink much because I need to leave and get ready for tonight. I think this case is a killer—no pun—and I want to be prepared. Sandy, take my coffee. Gotta go. Love you guys!" I gave the royal wave and left.

"See ya!" my girls yelled, clumsily.

The valet pulled up in my shiny black Mercedes coupe. I tipped him and drove up Broadway toward home. As I approached my garage, out from a bush jumped Mr. Corwin, shouting, "You can't leave me! You can't leave *me!*" Corwin pointed with his left hand while he struggled to hold an oversized construction hard hat on his head with the other. He wore a gray pinstriped suit jacket, blue button-down shirt, blue denim shorts, and red running shoes with his standard black panty hose. The hat was his protection from bad thoughts, or so he thought.

Mr. Corwin was my former stalker, a deviant patient who refused to accept the fact that my practice was now closed. I rolled down the window and shouted back, "I will call the police on your crazy ass if you come near my home again! Get the hell away from here!"

"You are a professional; you're not supposed to call me crazy!" Corwin shouted while running away.

As I drove under the iron gate into my underground parking lot, I had to laugh out loud. That lunatic was actually right; as his former therapist, it was inappropriate for me to call him crazy—to his face.

Jesus. Corwin today, Manuel tonight. The forecast for the coming year seems to be mysterious, murderous, with a touch of crazy. Damn ...

CHAPTER TWO

Whoever invented body language was full of shit. Manuel's gait told me nothing. I had recently read that experts consider body language inaccurate. Big surprise. *Is this hookup all business, business with a touch of interest, or a date with business as an excuse?* His movements gave no early clues.

"It's great to see you." Manuel stood more than six feet tall, dripping with overconfidence. His straight back and tight muscles made me feel safe and horny.

Ever since Manuel walked into the San Ramon police department to represent me back when it was assumed I was an accomplice to a murder, I had fought a blazing attraction to him. His gray-and-white Hugo Boss suit was no help in cooling that down. The high lapels and tailored cut gave in to his tight body. I was not only an expert in women's fashion, I also had an eye for men's fine tailoring, and this was it.

Nice. A clothes horse, like me.

We were seated in a booth at Tony's Beach Restaurant in San Francisco's Italian North Beach area. We slid on the soft leather seating under a white linen table cloth, positioned facing each other. "It's great to see you, too. Thanks for asking me to come. I love this place. It feels like the dining room of an Italian family." I smiled.

"That's true." Manuel gave a weak smile and looked around.

Three generations of Sepia-toned family photos lined the walls of the restaurant's hallways. The male waitstaff wore formal, short white server jackets with black slacks lined in hard creases. The women wore skirted versions of the same look. Their crisp demeanors mirrored their uniforms. Low lights and candles created a tender glow in the place. I thought the restaurant was a bit romantic for a business meeting, so I wondered what was really on Manuel's mind. He jumped into the facts of his case shortly after we ordered our drinks and removed any doubt of possible romance. Talking murder had cooled the mood.

"I have to tell you, I'm usually a bit cold and distant when I handle cases, but this one is different." Manuel's head hung. Then he looked up, as if startled. "Oh, I'm sorry; where are my manners? How are you? You've been through so much; I hope that leaving town for a while helped you rid yourself of some of last year's horrible events." He had slowed his speaking pace.

"No problem. I know how it feels to have something on your mind, and I don't need to revisit last year. The trip did actually help me to detox from all of the drama with Michael, a little. I handled a few other things while I was in Louisiana, but we can talk about that some other time. Manuel, I need a project. Despite my heroine status for helping to ultimately solve the case, last year's humiliation not only labeled me as the mistress in a murder scandal but also undermined any confidence in me as a family therapist. Cases no longer come from the courts or any other referrals. My years of success as a family therapist seem to have been forgotten and I'm still tainted with last year's news. Thankfully, I've invested well and have time to build a new career. Ironically, it seems it'll be related to my psychic gifts. If you would've told me this a few years ago, I would've laughed you out of this place. So, I need this as much as you do. I want to see if I can help with your case. Tell me what's going on." I stared into Manuel's eyes, and he nodded with understanding.

"Let me give you more background. We have a new attorney in our office, my partner—well, more accurately, my colleague—Yadira Lopez. You didn't meet her during your case, but she and I went to law school together at UCLA. She had her own practice for many years, but the pressures of running a business and doing client work got to her. She contacted me and asked to join our firm a few months ago, and I put in a good word for her. She brought a few high-profile clients with her. Yadira practices contract law." Manuel took a sip from his scotch on the rocks. I watched his lips hug the glass. I thought from the way Yadira's name left his lips that they might have had a past of some sort. The break gave me an opening. We both had waved off the waiter, who seemed eager to recite the evening's dinner specials.

"So it's her son who's in trouble?" I asked one question but actually had several more roaming within my head. Why was this so personal for Manuel? Were they really just friends? Why hadn't I heard about Yadira when he was saving my life last year? *OK, well during a murder trial may not have been the best time, but my other questions are valid.*

"Yeah, poor kid, Jorge Lopez. He's really her stepson. A brilliant young man who just turned nineteen. He got caught up in drugs. Not the cheap street stuff—cocaine. Yadira and her ex-husband provided him with the best of everything: good neighborhoods, schools, nannies, cars. You get the picture."

"Sure. He needed to feel the challenge of an edgier life," I added.

"Exactly. Well, right before his junior year at Cal State East Bay, Jorge was busted for possession of marijuana; not much more than an ounce, but the cops got him with intent to sell, so in addition to a five-hundred-dollar fine, he got six months. Yadira and her ex were heartbroken. They had managed to keep him out of the system during his cocaine addiction years by treatment and high-priced representation...me." Manuel offered a pitiful smile.

"So his time is almost up?" I asked.

"Well, it would've been. Two weeks ago, he woke up and found his cellmate dead. The funny thing is that he said they got along fine. No fights, no issues. He had no reason to kill the guy." Manuel waved off the waiter's second pass at our table, who made his frustration obvious.

"Is Jorge a tough guy type?" I asked.

"Far from it. He's a suburban kid, skinny and a bit quiet." He answered.

"Why do you think he's innocent, especially with the drugs and all? I mean are you sure or just thinking that way because of his stepmother?" I worked to mask slight jealousy.

"Sarah, I've been practicing criminal law a long time. It isn't only about the kid's history and me knowing his family, from the moment I started meeting with Jorge I saw a kid who got caught up experimenting with drugs who lacked the internal anger and violence usually required to kill. He doesn't have it in him." Manuel sat up straight to further make his point.

"I hear ya, but how in the world could anyone get into a cell and pull off a murder without being seen or heard? I guess I need to hear more about this." I was convinced there had to be much more to the story, but not necessarily convinced Manuel could be objective.

"Look, I know it sounds impossible, but I know he didn't do it." Manuel was firm.

"How did the cellmate die?" I asked.

"I wish I could tell you. We are waiting for the autopsy results and pushing the M.E.'s office. We can rule out the obvious things like gunshot or stabbed. No sound and no obvious marks on the body. You'll see that in the police reports." He stopped to take another drink.

"OK. I'm intrigued by this." I said.

"Yeah, I have all of the files for you. The more we learn, the more it seems apparent that this kid is being framed." Manuel stopped. He rarely looked vulnerable, but he appeared shaken. The man who had come to my rescue now needed me. I realized that asking me to work the case was not a way to throw my troubled ass a bone, and neither was it a cloaked reason to spend time with me; this case cut to Manuel's core. I was now involved, both to help Manuel and to find out why this case lived so deeply within his heart.

Manuel broke our impromptu silence to answer the waiter, now on his third trip to our booth to get our food orders.

"I could've gone for sushi." Manuel whispered.

"Me, too." I laughed. "But we're in the wrong part of the city." I smiled. We were deep in the heart of San Francisco's Italy. The waiter had heard us and was less amused. We fell back on vegetarian lasagna with shared steamed mussels as a starter. The sushi faux pas lightened the mood for a moment, but once our food arrived, we ate with no real commitment to the meal, his head filled with worry and mine with confusion.

The night ended with light conversation about our lives. As we waited at the valet stand for our cars, I sensed that Manuel wanted to kiss me, but he held back. His behavior was ambiguous. I hated that, but the attraction was building in me, and I wanted to learn more about him and the origins of his cautious behavior. My first murder case was about more than helping an allegedly innocent young man; it was my proving ground for success using my spirit gifts for something beyond a husband hunt. And with any luck, I would also solve the mystery of Manuel.

CHAPTER THREE

I let myself sleep in on Monday morning. The weekend had been heavy with old memories and new, complicated emotions. And more disturbing was the fact that my psychic visions were shady as fuck when I needed them to be clear. I had to have strong coffee and a Creole frittata in order to enter the day.

My bedroom had been renovated, post-Michael, into a new sanctuary. All traces of Michael had been removed before I left for Louisiana. I had a new, plush mattress, the kind that remembered your body for perfect support. The furniture was minimal but striking. A canopy bed dominated the room. It was a contemporary mahogany piece that looked as if it had come from the designer collection for a New Orleans bed-and-breakfast. An antique dressing table that for some reason reminded me of my late Aunt Cat, was angled in a corner of the room. My walls were a rich, shiny aubergine framed with six inch white baseboards. Accent pieces in turquoise and any other color that happened into my shopping journeys brought soft life and peace to the room. An unused polished brass gong sat in another corner; a bench at the foot of the bed was in a light pine wood with black-and-tan tufted zebra print. I had refused to place a rug on the striking wood floors. I did a quick straighten of my bed and went for the kitchen to begin cooking. It was late morning for me, nearly nine o'clock. The phone rang while I was pulling out eggs, cheese, shrimp and broccoli. My coffeemaker had already been pre-programmed to brew so I poured a cup.

"Sarah, what are you doing in a few weeks?" It was the unmistakably entitled voice of my Ma-ma, Bernice Jean-Louis. She and my late father had moved to California after World War II. They loved California, but kept the Creole culture alive in our traditions, food and her attempts to control the lives of me, my brother and sister.

"Hello to you, too." I laughed.

"Oh, silly. Hi, cher. I have a surprise," she announced in lackluster tone.

"Really? What kind of surprise?" I asked. "And I'm putting you on speaker while I cook and eat, Ma-ma."

"That's OK. Well, be nice. Your cousin Stacy is coming to California. Things aren't so good for her right now in Louisiana." Ma-ma cleared her throat. I stopped beating egg whites midstream for what I considered bad news.

"What? Oh, no. . . no. Don't tell me I have to see that horrible woman more often now? She's coming to my state? What happened, Louisiana kicked her out for overtaxing the marriage bureau?" I laughed, but hearing that my lifelong nemesis would be invading my space was in no way amusing.

"You see, that's the kind of thing I don't want you doing. Stacy has had a run of bad luck," Ma-ma lectured.

"Oh, puh-lease. What happened, some man's wife caught up with her?" I chuckled.

"No. Her Robert left her." Ma-ma's reluctant and humorless voice tossed the words out.

"What? The great man grabber? The one they all want? The hottie who gets any man she sets her mind to get, was dumped? Stacy's Robert left? Where did he find the nerve?" I laughed aloud. It was a great karmic return for the queen bitch. I thought about all the times Stacy had embarrassed me at family functions for attending solo, her disingenuous offers to fix me up with losers, and even the time our snipes had turned physical. *I'm not proud of that.*

"He ran off with another woman," Ma-ma whispered as if someone would hear us.

"Ah...hahahahahaha!" All I could do was laugh...from my gut.

"Stop that. Well, she'll stay with me for a while, but I want you to help her adjust to California. With Catin gone, she needs us. Remember she not long ago lost her mother. Maybe you can include her with your friends," Ma-ma instructed.

"Here's the problem: she ain't a friend to me—hell, she's barely family, according to the way she treats me. And what would she and my friends possibly have in common? They are real people. And, I'm working on a murder case now so I don't have time for this. But, whatever..." I resigned myself to bend to the power of Ma-ma's steel will.

She ignored me and my news about the murder case. "I have to go, but sounds like today is too soon for you to begin planning how you'll help Stacy. I'll call you later with a few suggestions." She quickly hung up.

Trite phrases ran through my mind like nervous ants. *Every dog has its day. What goes around comes around...*any and all expressions to define this moment. Stacy had spent a lifetime besting me in marriages and men, and now, for the first time in her life, she'd been dumped. I swallowed the last of my frittata, baffled.

Wow, wonder who that other woman is. Hell, I wonder how Robert medically managed to grow a pair of balls at his advanced age.

But Stacy's payback, which was almost as delicious as my Creole frittata, had to sit on my mental back burner. I had my new, exciting project and somewhere to go. Turning off my coffeemaker signaled that it was time to get ready for my first day on the job at Manuel's office. But while I cleared the dishes from my table, I stumbled under the force of one of my visions. Head-spinning nausea in flashing light swirled within my head. My inner eye focused on an image of myself walking down a dark, haunting hallway, no windows, no doors. I walked straight ahead and heard a voice in psychotic laughter. It was garbled. The vision ended, but the feeling of terror remained. It caused me to double-check locks and cover my windows. I felt sweat line my upper lip. The mind movies that helped me to steer my life and forecast its events kept my feet in two worlds: one physical and palpable, the other unseen but made manifest over time. What was this one? Loneliness? Confusion?

Captivity? *Dear God, I wish I could interpret these visions better.* I gave up and went for a hot, citrus-scented shower.

I stood in my familiar spot in the center of my opulent closet, a forty-plus version of myself at five years old on the first day of school. At five, my selections were fewer, but my intention was the same; I had to look special and be noticed. At forty-ish, I decided it was time for tweed. Black pencil skirt, red tank top, and a gray, black-and-camel tweed jacket. I wrapped a black scarf around my neck before leaving home, headed west to the iciness of San Francisco and my new crime-solving life.

God help me…

"Good morning, and welcome to Slovensky, Hicklestein, Mason, and Cabrera. You must be Ms. Jean-Louis?" The receptionist asked, despite knowing me from my many visits to the office a year before. I nodded yes. She was a twenty-something cliché of a woman with blazing, undeniably dyed red hair. The image was set aflame by her electric blue blazer over a lime-green dress. *I understand now why the old-school law firms insisted support staff wear uniforms or uniformed colors.* The nameplate on her desk read Kelly Grayson.

"Yes. Thank you, Kelly." I smiled.

"I'll ring Mr. Cabrera's assistant and she'll come out and take you to your office. Just a minute," she affirmed. Manuel and I had agreed I would have an office at his building while maintaining my base with Jean at my offices in Old Oakland.

"Good morning." I greeted Janelle, Manuel's assistant, who also knew me from my many hours in their offices a year earlier, the year of Michael. I owed Manuel and his firm my life and freedom. I hoped working on this case could at least in some way pay them back, in addition to the large invoice I had already paid them.

Janelle stood like a redwood in five-inch, black high heels and a gray suit with a collared, white shirt. "Great to see you again, Dr.

Jean-Louis, and it's so wonderful to have you onboard. Please follow me to the hall on the right." Janelle made a sweeping motion pointing to the hallway as if it were a game show door of prizes. I then led the way. I never understood why people who worked or lived at a place would have you walk in front of them, when you couldn't possibly know which way to go. For this reason, Janelle had to take the lead, halfway. She stopped at a large office overstuffed with everything: a huge desk, chairs, books, supplies, a hidden bar—*thank goodness*—and two phones. *What? This is nice.*

"Mr. Cabrera asked that we provide you with this office, and please let me know if there's anything you need that's not here." Janelle smiled and left before I could answer. She was a frosty type.

I sat in the soft leather chair and before I could enjoy a school-girl swivel, a voice that had obviously been intimate with too many cigarettes called my name, sort of. I turned around and thought I was being visited by a 1970s hologram. Standing shorter than the average man, I guessed about five-foot-seven, fifty-something years old, with smushed bagel showing as he chewed, and wearing a coffee-stained tie was Manuel's private investigator.

"Ms. John-Louis. Hi there. I'm Caswell, the former NYPD detective you'll be partnering with to work investigations. I was told that I bring the police know-how, and you bring the, uh, hocus-pocus, right?" Caswell was unaware that he was offensive. He looked like a TV sitcom detective wearing a plastic looking Columbo-esque raincoat. His suit was brown, worn shiny. He finished off this look with a white, button-less collared shirt. The tie was too awful to remember; it seemed to be a confusion of horizontal stripes attempting to shadow each other in degrees of brown and green, not to be confused with the coffee stain brown. In my view he was a walking fashion felony.

"Uh, good to meet you, Caswell. If you can call me Jean-Louis instead of John-Louis, we'll be fine. As for the hocus-pocus, you have a lot to learn about psychic intuition. The way it works is…" I was cut off.

"Yeah, yeah, we got time for all that. Grab your notebook and head to the conference room. Manuel and Yadira want to meet with us." Caswell waved his notebook as if shooing me out of the door.

I'll deal with you later, Jersey boy. I could walk on Caswell's accent, but that didn't bother me; his attitude was of more concern. I followed him into the conference room and it looked like a place Manuel would work; attractive, expensive and not especially warm. I could tell the firm had used a top shelf designer; there was the over-used attempt to create an office personality with themes. This theme seemed to be stone, marble and aqua colored glass. The glass conference table had a marble base of white and gray with executive Eames-like chairs of gray leather. One side of the room was all glass, showing the office cubicles and hallways and the three walls were a soft gray. The artwork supported the stone and glass theme with abstract art created using framed stone and aqua colored glass. One wall sported a white credenza with full bar and coffee service. I took a quick mental assessment of the people sitting around the conference table. I guessed that the olive-skinned, dark-haired woman in the pale blue Dolce & Gabbana suit that I almost bought the weekend before was Yadira. She seemed to make it a point not to look up as I walked into the conference room. She waited until Manuel's introduction to acknowledge me. Her eyes seemed familiar. She maintained her composure as we talked, clinically, about her stepson's case. I hadn't met young Jorge yet, but I was already hurting for him.

"OK, everyone, before we go around the table for updates, I want to introduce a new team member. Everyone but Yadira and Caswell met Dr. Sarah Doucette Jean-Louis last year when we represented her in the Michael Rochon case. This year, she joins us to add special insight into our investigations. Sarah, you know the team." Manuel looked at home at the head of the table tapping a pen, in charge.

I looked around the room and smiled at the two paralegals, as well as assistant, Janelle and doofus, PI Caswell.

"Sarah, please meet Yadira Anda Lopez; her stepson is our client, Jorge Lopez."

Yadira managed a faint smile in my direction. She wore light makeup, and her wavy hair was pulled back tightly into a low ponytail.

"I want to thank you, Sarah for helping with Jorge's case. It's a comfort to me to know that all of you believe in him." The tone of

Yadira's voice was nearly as deep as mine but, frankly, had a more mellow quality to it.

I had to say something, so I made a promise I could only hope to keep. "We will get to the truth, I promise you."

Manuel looked at me and smiled. "Let's get to our updates. What do we have?"

One of the paralegals started. She gave an overview of the police report. "The report stated that at one o'clock the morning of June sixteenth, Jorge Lopez was screaming for the jailers to come to his cell. The suspect said he woke up to find his cellmate's eyes open, but no signs of life. The cellmate, Timothy Reston, was confirmed dead by prison authorities, unknown cause of death at the time. Inmate Lopez stated that he had not had an argument or fight with cellmate. He had fallen asleep, he thought, around nine o'clock. Sheriff's deputies were called, and an investigation was opened. The following week, Jorge Lopez was named the primary suspect in the case." Yadira steadied her glance. She was a beautiful woman with a near masculine jawline. Ironically, it made her more attractive. I assumed Manuel thought so, too.

Caswell spoke first. "We have got to get our hands on the cause of death. Seems to be taking too long."

"I agree with you and we're all over that; right?" Manuel looked at the two paralegals.

The report reader spoke up, "Absolutely. We are calling the medical examiner's office, daily."

"How detailed is the description of the body? Any visible wounds? Blood clotting? Anything?" I was all in.

Yadira looked at me briefly, but turned to face Manuel as she spoke.

"We have all asked those same questions, Sarah. Nothing obvious. We'll have to wait for the autopsy report."

Aw hell, yeah. They had a thing. I can tell.

"I'd like to see it as soon as you guys have it. I'm not an MD, but I'm greatly familiar with medical reports." I spoke to the paralegals and ended my sentence with a half-smile aimed at Yadira.

"Definitely." Manuel affirmed.

"And I know that I'm the stepmother, but I want to be included in all updates and communications. I need to see all emails and files, any information about the case." Yadira insisted.

I think we're having a contest, but I'm not sure what we're competing for or about.

"Thank you. Also as a reminder, the cops have been all over this case, trying to question everybody. Be careful about answering any questions because you never know who you're talking to. We have to keep our heads up on this one. I have managed to keep them away from Jorge for the most part." Manuel looked around the room.

Caswell jumped in. "Yeah, the cops are trying to close a case and they won't take the time always to look for all the details. They think it's Jorge and talking them out of that is damn near impossible."

"Exactly. Thanks, Caswell. Now I want to go over a few more items." Manuel glanced at a mountainous bundle of legal pads in front of him, and I could tell we were in for a long-winded recitation. While all eyes were fixed on him, I looked at Yadira and was taken aback by what I saw. She stared at me in a strange way. And when she noticed I had caught her, she smirked and defiantly gave a smile.

You bitch! You just became suspicious in my mind. Not sure what you may have done, but my eyes are now on you, Yadira.

Even though I was brought in to save her stepson, she seemed quite comfortable spewing hateful glances at me. While Manuel's voice trailed into the background, I searched my mental history to see if I had had any dealings with Yadira in the past. I came up empty. I felt sure that I had seen her before because those eyes were familiar.

Manuel continued. "So Janelle, let's make sure that we update Sarah's files today."

Before the meeting ended, I recalled where I had seen Yadira's eyes: they were in the vision that had come to me only days before the meeting. Cold and evil, they were eyes that sent chills through me. But there was no way I could share this with Manuel until I had some factual information. I made the decision that the idiot detective, Caswell, would be my ally. Through him I would expose her. I just didn't know of what or how…yet.

"Everyone, you'll be notified when we'll all meet again as a full team. Until then, continue to work in your smaller groups as we advance the case. Thank you."With that, Manuel ended the meeting.

The warm tickle of panic settled into the pit of my stomach as the realization hit me that although I was an evolving gifted, psychic intuitive, I hadn't learned how to control my visions before my dear mentor, Aunt Cat, had passed on. Aunt Cat had uncanny command of psychic intuition and could call visions to her. But unless I learned to do that, I would face challenges in trying to help Manuel or anyone in solving crimes or using my gifts for any other good. I made up forgettable excuses for leaving early and selected the parking garage button at the elevator bay. I had decided to drive into the city my first day rather than take BART, our rail service, for no particular reason; but once in my car and out of the garage, I was glad I decided to drive. I needed to make a quick phone call in the privacy of my car. I had to talk to Ma-ma immediately, because only she could help me.

Three rings blared over my speaker system.

"Hello?"

"It's me, Ma-ma."

"Oh. Hi, Sarah. Is everything all right?"

"In a way things are OK, but in a way...not. I need your help." It was as if I could feel the pleasure ooze through the other end of the phone. It wasn't often I asked Ma-ma for opinions or help, because we had little, other than our DNA, in common.

"Really? In what way?" she asked.

"Ma-ma, I think that I may have bitten off more than I can handle. I just left my first meeting at Manuel's office. I'm supposed to use my gifts to help him solve a crime and free his client. This is the first case where I'll intentionally use my gifts, but you know how my visions work—they just come to me, randomly. If I'm going to work on cases, I need to be able to call on answers like Aunt Cat used to do. You know what I mean?"

"I know. I wondered when you'd realize that, but I didn't want to say anything because I know how you argue with me. You'll need some kind of what Catin called a treatment to change how you get the visions," Ma-ma explained.

"A treatment?" I asked.

"Yeah. I don't know all about it, but let me make a couple of calls back home. Now, we may have to go to Louisiana for this..."

"Ma-ma, we'll go. Just let me know when. I've accepted that this could be my new life, and I need to go all the way. I expect this might be something peculiar to me, but hell, I'm game." I chuckled.

"Don't make fun. This is serious stuff, Sarah." Ma-ma chastised.

"I know. I get it. Just let me know what I need to do. Will you go with me?"

"Of course. I'll call you later tonight with what we'll need to do." Ma-ma hung up.

This should be wild.

Minutes later I had arrived at my office parking garage in Old Oakland and climbed the beautiful spiral stairs to the Jean-Louis offices. The spiral staircase is an Old Oakland signature. In the late 1800s, the area marked the move of the central business area from Oakland's waterfront inland. Back then it was a vibrant downtown center. As with many older centers, it saw decline and later, restoration. Rows of beautifully renovated Victorians in classy monochromes and a city center that intimately blends history with the diversity of positive growth, make up the contemporary Old Oakland. When I started my business, it was the only place I wanted my offices to be located. As I entered the glass front office door, I could hear Jean organizing as only she can.

"Hi, Jean. How's it going?"

"All is well here. Did you make it to Manuel's meeting as planned?" she asked.

"Yes. Here are the notes and files from it. We can go over them in more detail later. I'm still wrapping my head around how we will support this new work," I said.

"While you get us ready, I'm still reorganizing the office. We had a lot to move out into storage—old patient files that you said we need to hold on to. I'm making up new files so we're prepared for this different type work," Jean said.

"That's a good plan." I watched Jean in yet another of her many matching pantsuits, this one beige with a pink shirt. I hated those things, but she loved order and symmetry. Jean was my alter ego and stability in a life of rapid evolution. Jean was all things predictable. Her hair cut reminded me of the short hairdo's of the early 1960s, no strand had its freedom. Tall and slender, Jean was of medium brown skin, dark brown hair and nothing that shouted, 'look at me.' Her glasses were the wireframes that you see on people who don't want to bother choosing unique frames. An attractive woman with a wide nose, generous lips and no real distinct features, she wore little make up, only a touch of blush and lip gloss. Me and the girls joked that if we ever got her drunk, we'd take her for an eyebrow wax. At 45, she seemed much older than me. She had married young, had no children and was settled. She traveled the middle of the road in life avoiding drama other than working for me. She had a compartment for everything, even her lunch box had food sections. Her desk had a place for everything while I often had to crawl under mine to find a pen. I thanked my stars for an assistant who filled in the blanks of all of my weaknesses and remained with me through the disorder and dangers of my unusual life.

She walked into my office holding a notepad. "You've had a few calls. Manuel's office called to say he'd like you to go to his meeting with Jorge so you can talk with the young man. The meeting is set up for tomorrow morning. I will put this on your calendar."

"Sounds good. I want to get a good look at this kid. They are convinced he's being framed, but I need to see that for myself," I said.

"That makes sense. Now, if you haven't made lunch plans for today, you got a call with an invitation from an old friend—a former patient, that is." She raised her eyebrows.

We said the name together: "Corwin!" And laughed.

"Oh damn!" I shook my head.

CHAPTER FOUR

Reluctantly, and with a sense of obligation, I met deviant, socio-path, and my onetime patient, Corwin, at one of those trendy retro diners in downtown Oakland, appropriately named "The Diner." Our booth was nearly swallowed up by Corwin's latest large, thought-protector hat. We both ordered french fries smothered in ketchup with black coffee.

"You owe me." Corwin didn't seem to realize his presumed author-ity was undermined by his head gear. He wore his usual expensive suit, this one in black with a white shirt, faint silver-colored pocket square and matching tie. But the hat he had chosen on this day to protect his mind from evil messages was reminiscent of those worn at either the Kentucky derby or a black church on Easter Sunday. It was huge and lime green, with feathers, bows, and intrusive netting. But he said he needed hats to keep him from committing evil acts, so I continued to tolerate his proclivities.

"Owe you? In what possible way?" I asked.

"I tried to protect you from that so-called fiancé of yours. I don't know how you let yourself become engaged to that criminal, you are supposed to know better. I knew he was bad news. I would've killed him for you, you know." Corwin's casual mention of taking a life was alarming but not totally out of character.

"Uh. Let's not talk about killing. And since you didn't actually save me from Michael, I don't really owe you. You know that I'm no longer in practice and can't be your therapist. But before I call the police about your stalking issues, what exactly do you want with me?" I was curt.

Corwin looked down at his red running shoes for a long pause. He held both of his index fingers to his mouth and seemed to be carefully planning his response.

"I need a reason to live." I didn't expect what I heard and he continued with clarity and sincerity that was unusual for him. "I need a purpose. I need to be useful. I know that I am a disturbing creature, but I can't help it. Still, I need to feel I am contributing to something on this earth. I've tried suicide several times, as you know, and I'm not even good at that. Dr. Sarah, I need to be good at something." He held his jaw tightly while his steel-blue eyes became crystal with tears. I found myself feeling sorry for this highly disturbed and textbook sick man. But something in his eyes broke through my fears and into my heart. I threw him an unrehearsed bone.

"I think I may have something you can do." I almost wanted to swallow the words, but they leaped from my mouth before I could rewind them. And like the child who is always picked last for kickball who finally got a break, Corwin's eyes lit up with the excitement of validation. "You do?" he asked.

I hesitantly spoke the words I had immediately regretted, but would later appreciate. "Yes. Since you're good at stalking, do you think you could follow a few people for me over the course of an investigation?" I asked.

Corwin boasted, "Hell, I can follow people for weeks, and they'd never see me."

He was right about his ability to follow people for weeks, but discretion was hardly his strong suit; the colorful variety of hats and his inability to keep a secret made him as obvious as the black panty hose he insisted upon wearing over his pasty-white legs. My hope was that his strangeness made others consider him irrelevant, and they would say anything or do anything in his presence.

"And look at it this way, after my uncle died leaving me an inheritance I have even more money than I had when you met me, so you don't have to pay me." Corwin flashed a privileged smile.

"You bet your ass I won't pay you." I smiled back. I knew I could use him in the Lopez case. I didn't know all of the specifics of his assignment yet, but I was sure I wanted him to follow Yadira. I had a strong feeling that the grieving stepmother wasn't who Manuel thought she was, and I had to prove it. Hopefully, this stalker-investigator crazy man could help me to do that. Our meeting ended with Corwin ecstatic and me wondering what the hell I was thinking.

I returned to my office for a few hours, where I filled Jean in on my unexpected offer to Corwin. Despite nearly choking on her own spit, Jean accepted the news with an "OK. I guess we'll see." I smiled and poured us two shots of vodka. This marked the beginning of a new tradition to celebrate the end of particularly challenging days with one vodka shot to close the office and head for home.

As I turned the key in my front door, I could hear my home phone ringing. I caught it in time.

"Hello?"

"I thought I was going to miss you. You sure took a long time to answer."

"Hi, Ma-ma." Why did my mother have to give commentary on nearly every call rather than just say, "Glad I got you" or "Oh, did you just get home?"

"Anyway, I think I have what you need." Ma-ma was proud to be in the advisor role usually held by the late Aunt Cat.

"This is great, Ma-ma. I'm listening."

She began explaining a mystery-filled Louisiana visit that would change my life forever. Ma-ma's information and our subsequent trip to Louisiana would provide the last key piece to the missing puzzle of my spiritual gifts. Unfortunately, the information wouldn't dramatically change the nature of our relationship, but somehow it seemed all was as it should have been in that way, as well.

"Sarah, you may or may not remember your Aunt Cat talking about a woman called Miss Lorena. Miss Lorena is second only to Catin in spirit gifts and spells. When Catin was too busy or unavailable to help people around there, they would go to Miss Lorena. Well, she's still alive. She's in her late nineties. I talked to her daughter and told her the situation. They're so proud of you, using spirit gifts to solve crimes. They say you're giving spirit gifts a good name after so much negative lies have been told about voodoo and our culture. Anyway, I told them that your gift is haunting you and you have trouble calling on them to get information when you need it. Her daughter said Miss Lorena can help you with that and give you a treatment for that. But you have to go to her house for the treatment. It can't be done by phone. I didn't think so."

"That's not a problem. When can she see us?" I asked.

"She's old, so we better hurry. You know what I mean." Ma-ma spoke in a hushed tone.

"I know. I'll get flights for some time this week or next week. Will that work for you?" I asked.

"Yeah. Let's move fast on this. I'm happy about this new work you're doing, too. I want to see you continue with it, mon cher."

"Ok. I'll call you with our flight itinerary when I get it from Jean. Thank you so much, Ma-ma."

"Thank you, Sarah for coming to me. Bye." She hung up. That was Ma-ma. She held a tender moment for about twenty-seconds and abruptly cut it off. I had to smile about that. My next call was to Jean.

"Hello," Jean answered.

"Hi Jean. I hate to call you at home right after work, but I need two things in a hurry. Ma-ma and I have to go to Louisiana, but not Franklin this time. We need to go a town called New Iberia. We'll need to fly into Lafayette and rent a car. Let's do a two-day stay, flying back the third day sometime this week or next week, but the sooner the better. Also, because I have this unexpected trip, I will need to introduce Corwin and Caswell so they can start working together. I know…the clash of the clueless…but I have to put those two in sync with each other. Remember, I added Corwin to this strange team I'm creating."

"Yeah, how could I forget?" Jean snickered.

I gave a light chuckle, too. "Work with me, Jean. Well, I think the sooner we get them on to Yadira, the better. So I need a meeting with the two of them before I leave for Louisiana," I said.

"No problem. I'm on it." Jean listened.

"If possible, maybe they can meet me after I come from visiting Jorge with Manuel in the morning?" I asked.

"I'll see and then call you back when I have all of this set up." Jean said.

"Thanks, Jean. I'll wait to hear from you. Try to set up a lunch at The Diner when you can reach the duo."

As soon as I hung up the phone, my head swirled at a dizzying pace in preparation for one of my damn visions. It came with the predictable nausea and the taste of rotten meat on my tongue. In black and white I saw an uncomfortably close image of those evil eyes again. They were almond-shaped, catlike, and cold. But this time they rang familiar. They were definitely the eyes of Yadira. They blinked and tightened as if staring directly into mine, they released a few tears and turned still. The blinking stopped and there was a blank stare. The vision dissolved into a mist. I may not have been able to fully interpret visions at that point, but I knew when trouble was on the way. I shuddered. Yadira's eyes frightened me with their chilly intensity. I seemed to be a target. I decided to draw my visions. I hadn't done this before, but it occurred to me that if I added drawings to the notes for the case, it might help with organizing the clues. I was willing to try everything to build this sinister story. As I finished putting the lashes on Yadira's horrid eyes, Jean called back.

"Dr. Sarah, I got them. Corwin and Caswell will be at The Diner tomorrow at twelve thirty. I'm still working on the trip arrangements. I'll send you an e-mail with details later tonight."

"Thanks, Jean. You're the best."

A dreamless sleep came easily that night and the morning rushed in with the anxiety of a trip to the San Francisco county jail to meet the young man whose life I signed on to save. I pulled an intentionally drab olive-colored suit and rare white shirt from my closet to achieve appropriate jail visitor attire, gulped my coffee and drove to meet Manuel in front of the building.

"Well, you look different." Manuel smiled and greeted me with a kiss on the cheek.

"What? It's the county jail. I brushed up on the dress code for visitors."

"No, it's that even during the trial last year, you never wore such plain clothes. It's a little bit funny."

"Well, you look like you work at a funeral home, you know." We both laughed.

"I guess I deserved that." Manuel chuckled and his face quickly straightened. "OK. About Jorge. He's nervous and scared so please go slow with him."

"Of course." I meant the words at the time I said them, but once inside sitting with the quiet young man, my patience ran short.

"Jorge, this is Sarah Jean-Louis. She is helping with the investigation." Manuel introduced us. The thin rail of a man looked younger than his 19 years. He almost seemed malnourished with his caved in chest and lack of body fat. His nervousness was understandable, but the way he looked side to side almost made him seem suspicious or dishonest. Once he spoke, I could tell he was just a confused and frightened kid.

"Hi." He looked side to side and then down. "Uh, thank you and all."

"You are welcome. Please, tell me what happened. I read the report but I want to hear from you everything that happened that night." I began. Manuel let me take the lead since it was my first time meeting Jorge.

"Well, uh, what do you want to know?" He spoke almost in a whisper.

"What happened in your cell."

"Like, uh, from when? When I got here?" He asked. His head was still down and he looked up with wide, long-lashed eyes.

"No, dear. The night you found your cellmate dead." My voice held a hint of testy.

"Oh. Uh, he wasn't breathing and uh . . . ." He began.

"Jesus, kid! Do you want us to help you or not? Paint a fucking picture of the whole night. That night. No other night. The killing they are accusing you of. . . . jeez." I bulleted back. *So much for patience.*

Manuel came to his rescue. "Sarah means, she needs to hear the whole story from you. I know you've told me everything, but she needs to be able to hear from you something I might have missed or not paid attention to; understand?"

"Oh, uh. OK. I got it." He shook his head yes.

"Well, I had already been here for months and they put this new guy in here about two weeks before he died. They said my other cell-mate was released. He didn't talk much, but the new guy, Timothy Reston, he talked a lot." Jorge steadied himself in his seat. He seemed to be more comfortable telling his story.

"What did he tell you?" I asked.

"The first day they put him in here, like, he told me he was an informant and wouldn't have to stay in here long. He was kinda bragging. He said he always was let out pretty fast." Jorge looked around to see if he was being overhead. The green-walled, smudged up visitor room was hardly private. Phone bays of bullet-proof glass and jailers everywhere nurtured a feeling of paranoia.

"Did he tell you about any cases he was working on?" I pushed.

Jorge hesitated and then said, "No. Nothin'." He looked at Manuel.

"Jorge, I've told you before we can't help if you're hiding something." Manuel pressed. It was apparent this was a source of frustration.

Sweat formed on Jorge's top lip and his calm escaped. His shaky nervousness returned. "You don't understand, there's all kind of talk in here and no secrets. They could kill me in here and you can't do nothin' about it. I don't know anything, I just know I can't go on in here. I can't. I gotta get outta here." Tears flowed from Jorge's eyes. He rubbed his eyes with his hands. And at that moment my impatience with his shy communicative style and nervous silence halted. I got myself in check remembering when I was suspected of a crime and how I felt helpless and paralyzed at times. I wanted to hug the poor kid but I couldn't touch him, so I did the next best thing. I comforted him.

"Just take your time and try to tell us everything you remember, sights, sounds, smells and all of it." He shook his head yes. "And look at me, Jorge." I pointed to my eyes. "Yes, Ms. Sarah?" I put my hand on the glass and he put his hand to mine, "I promise you, we will find the truth and get your ass out of here. I promise you, I will use everything in my power. You will be free." My eyes filled with tears that I refused to let fall. Manuel grabbed my other hand and smiled.

"Jorge, let's just talk it through so that Sarah can listen for things others can't see or hear. She has a gift." He said. Jorge sniffled, relaxed and repeated his story. I could tell this boy was not a killer. From what Jorge told us, it seemed obvious that Timothy was intentionally placed in his cell; but who had the power to make that happen and why?

This is exactly why I need to get my psychic act in order.

I left Manuel with Jorge at the jail and went straight to my lunch meeting of my rag-tag team, Corwin and Caswell. It was important for me to arrive first so that I could choose a booth at The Diner with privacy, away from ears and eyes. I had hoped Caswell would show up first, and he did, at 12:15 p.m. I needed time to explain and describe his new partner to him: bizarre-hat-wearing, panty-hose-clad Corwin.

"Detective. Have a seat." I gestured. "I'm glad you're early; we have a lot to cover."

"Ya see, Ms., uh, John-Louis, er, John-Louie, or Jean-Louie...I think we need to start at the beginning in this case." Caswell looked confident as he rotated his right hand in uneven circles.

"But you see, detective, that's the problem; we don't know what the beginning is yet." I had lost patience with this...relic. He didn't appear to listen well and questioned my credibility.

"You don't seem to wanna recognize anything that didn't come from your, er, hocus-pocus-try, but there's a clear beginning," Caswell persisted.

"First of all, if you use the phrase 'hocus-pocus' one more time when referring to my psychic intuitive gifts, I'll use them to give you a suspicious rash no doctor can cure.

"Hey! You can do that?" Caswell looked skeptical, but concerned. "You don't gotta be cruel."

"Well, you don't gotta be so loose with the insults." We both smiled at my attempt to mimic his accent.

"I didn't know I was insulting ya. I guess I'm a bit rough around the edges. Sorry, doc." He smiled.

A waitress finally made way to our booth. It seemed she had walked right out of central casting; shirt dress, apron, name on shirt and pad with pencil.

"What you want, hun?" she asked.

"I'll take a coffee and french fries. And we have another one coming."

"OK." She nodded while writing my order. "And for you?" She turned to Caswell.

"I'll have a BLT, a bag of chips, two of them chocolate chip cookies and a glass of water." Caswell opened his napkin and stuffed it in his shirt collar. I winced at his lack of table manners, but continued the conversation.

"My point is, if you think the beginning of the case began with the murder, I believe you're mistaken. This situation began with the initial *thought* to commit the murder. To pass it off as a typical jailhouse brawl would be wrong. And you won't find the culprit without my so-called hocus-pocus, because sometimes it's what you can't see that matters more than what you can see. Now, let's start over and talk what we know." It felt good to clear the air with Caswell and to focus on the work to clear Jorge.

"OK, OK. It'll take some gettin' used to, but I'll work with any information you give me," Caswell agreed.

"Great. Let's start with something that may shock you. I think Yadira is somehow involved. I have a bad feeling about her. And I've noticed the way she looks at me in the meetings. Something's not right about her." I risked putting my suspicions out there without real physical evidence and was caught off guard by Caswell's response.

"I never trusted that woman. Here's some background for you. Hubby's first wife died in childbirth. He raised the kid by himself until little Jorge was about ten years old. Word is Jorge hated the evil stepmother and that could've started his drug problems a long time ago.

Manuel doesn't know I know this yet 'cause, as you see, he has a kinda soft spot for Yadira. I couldn't bust his bubble with no facts." Caswell nodded. "I got some gossip from a few sources who know the dad." The "soft spot" remark cut through me. I realized I was more fond of Manuel than I was ready to admit to myself.

"I have someone who can start following her and report all of her movements to you. In fact, he's coming here today, because I wanted to introduce you to him. I'm glad you showed early so I can give you some important background information about him." I was sheepish.

"Uh-oh. What's wrong?" Caswell showed off his good instincts.

"Full disclosure, Mr. Corwin is a former therapy patient of mine and is prone to mood swings and histrionics." I waited for a reaction.

"My guess is he's cheap. Aw, what the hell, we always had a few sickos on the force," Caswell blew it off.

"Try free. He doesn't need money, he's crazy but loaded. But, the other thing…" I hesitated.

"There's another thing?" he asked.

"Yeah, he wears different types of hats to protect his brain from voices he hears in his head. The voices tell him to do bad things, and he says the hats help him. And he wears panty hose." I rushed through the explanation.

"Hats? Panty hose? Geez-Louise. A whack-a-doodle. Anything else?" Caswell shook his head.

"Well, that's enough, ain't it?" He laughed at my second attempt to mock his New Jersey accent.

As if on cue, Corwin walked in, looking every bit the businessman in a gray pinstriped suit, with the exception of a large-brimmed, floppy blue hat and a toothy grin. "Hi everyone; are we ready to talk about our case?" he announced from the door while he walked to our booth.

"Shut up, you idiot. Remember our work is confidential." I was frustrated before we even began.

"Oy vey." Caswell gasped, slapped his hand to his cheek, and rolled his eyes to the ceiling.

"Oh, OK." Corwin made a shush motion with a finger in front of his lips, oblivious to the true nature of his offense.

Caswell and I brought Corwin up to speed on our suspicions about Yadira.

"I have to leave town for a few days and I need you guys to begin surveillance on her while I'm away. Hopefully, you can build a file for when I return."

"No problem." Caswell said. "I'll work with Corwin here on structuring the surveillance."

Corwin nodded his head in agreement. "We're on it."

"Sounds like a good plan." I said.

And with that, my motley crew of investigators took shape. I thought it best to keep the news of this team from Manuel, initially. He didn't need to know everything. And I needed ramp-up time to find the right way to explain them to him.

CHAPTER FIVE

A week after I had put my team in place, I was on a plane with Ma-ma. I had no idea what to expect from this short adventure to the backwoods of rural Louisiana for a deep spiritual quest. Ma-ma and I landed in Lafayette several hours and two stops after we had boarded in Oakland. Thanks to first-class seats and smooth vodka, I was in a good mood. Ma-ma quickly fell asleep on one glass of cabernet. While she slept, I looked at my diminutive mother. Her olive-colored skin, keen features, deep set eyes and soft, wavy hair screamed Louisiana Creole. And although she had never worked outside of our home, when traveling or going to a restaurant she always wore knit suits. She was wearing a navy blue one for the flight. It had a straight skirt, short jacket and belt. Her blouse was white and collared. Her tiny feet were in navy pumps with kitten heels. Her hand clasped a cotton handkerchief while she slept. A collage of Ma-ma moments ran through my head, but were quickly eclipsed by the sour note of an unplanned vision. My head throbbed and I had to close my eyes from the pain. I saw myself driving, happily around the Bay Area. It was a sunny day that rapidly turned gray and dark. In the darkness I saw colorful lights and the lights blinded me, I couldn't stop driving, and I couldn't see where I was going, I only saw massive light that covered the rest of the scenery. I started to moan and remembered I was on a plane with people around. I opened my eyes, felt a pang of worry for Jorge and looked to see if anyone had heard me.

I hope Miss Lorena can stop this shit!

Eventually, I went to sleep until Ma-ma woke me. "We're about to land, cher." She yawned.

"Well, Sarah, let's get the rental car and get down to New Iberia." Ma-ma stretched; her four-foot-ten frame stood effortlessly in the short space under the overhead compartments. It seemed to take forever to leave the plane. Finally, we checked in at the rental car counter and worked on our game plan.

"Do we want to go down to Franklin to see family or friends while we're here?" I asked.

"I think you need to focus on this mission, Sarah. Why don't we visit Miss Lorena and skip the others, Stacy or anyone else, this trip?" Ma-ma suggested.

"I think you're right, Ma-ma. I don't really know what this experience will be, so I need to concentrate on the reason we came here. Even little Brandon is being cared for, so there's no reason to see him this visit, either." Brandon was Michael's son from a late girlfriend. I provided financial support for the boy after his mother died and her family all but abandoned him. I arranged for him to attend the best private schools and, working with an attorney, he now had more money than her family, all protected in a trust.

It took about an hour after landing before Ma-ma and I started our travel down the dark roads to our hotel in New Iberia. A larger town than Ma-ma's home town of Franklin, New Iberia had a population of more than thirty thousand. The home of Tabasco hot sauce and sugar plantations, it was like a south Louisiana postcard of colonial mansions, with signature white columns and two-lane roads lined with large, angling oak trees draped in Spanish moss casting gloomy shadows from the streetlights.

"I think all I want to do is get into that bed tonight." Ma-ma yawned.

"I know. I'm too tired to think of anything else." Miraculously we found the hotel from the poorly lit roads, and once inside our room, sleep came quickly.

The distant crow of a rooster served as a familiar rural wake-up call for Ma-ma and me as the sun peeked through rich burgundy drapery and sheer, embroidered curtain panels. I couldn't help but be a little nervous about what would be my first spiritual "treatment." And I had no idea what that meant.

"I told Miss Lorena we would see her between nine and ten this morning. It's seven o'clock now, so let's get dressed and find some chicory coffee," Ma-ma insisted. In the country, it was common to set appointments with a time range rather than a time-certain. That irritated the Type A part of my personality, but it was the way they did things, so I assimilated.

"Good idea. I want to check out the café downstairs. Maybe we can find a croissant, too?" I began to pull clothes out of my suitcase. Ma-ma nodded in agreement as she pulled toiletries from her luggage.

Stuffed with strong French Creole chicory coffee and buttery croissants, Ma-ma and I set out for the adventure to Miss Lorena and the spirit work that would move me to a higher level in my gift of visions. As with many small towns, some roads had signage and others had to be identified as 'the-place-where-Joe-used-to-have-a-shoe-shop' by locals. Despite that, we managed to find the little yellow and white Victorian wood frame house tucked into a forest-like area about ten miles outside of the New Iberia city limits. We walked up three uneven, wood steps and as I lifted my hand to turn the old fashioned, painted metal doorbell, we heard a rich voice weighted in the sing-song patois of a Creole accent that said, "I'm so glad ya got down, yeah cher. Mais, come on in. Da door, it be open, yeah."

As I slowly pushed the squeaky screen door, my heart raced with nervous anticipation. Ma-ma was right behind me as we walked in. We entered the living room and were met by the smell of simmering red beans propped up with onions, bay leaf, thyme and andouille sausage. My home cook's nose could identify each ingredient down to the herbs and spices. As I looked around the room, I could feel a presence of something larger than the house or any of us. The creaking of the wood floor signaled the entrance of Miss Lorena.

"Oh, it's so good to see da bode o' ya, yeah." The deep chocolate face of Miss Lorena was wrinkle-free and framed in white, crinkly hair. Her dress was an old house dress of faded green and beige paisley print. Miss Lorena was a large woman who stooped over as she walked, likely from her huge legs and generous backside. She had swollen ankles that looked painful to me, and her feet slid across the floor in brown cloth slippers with backs worn flat. She grabbed my ice princess of a mother in a bear hug and then moved on to do the same to me. It startled us.

"Oh, Bernice. I haven't seen't ya in so long, bebe. I miss ya sistah Catin so, so much. Oh, Catin was a magical woman, yeah. Oh, da gifts of Catin, oh, no one got dem, no." She shook her head.

"Noooo, noo. That's right." Ma-ma proudly contributed to the praise of her late sister, Aunt Cat. "And wouldn't you know, my Sarah inherited the gift. Of all the grandchirren, only Sarah. Praise God." Ma-ma's accent always re-surfaced when we visited Louisiana.

Miss Lorena turned her attention back to me. "Oh, Ti-Sarah. Das a good blessin', yeah." She hugged me again.

"Uh, thank you, so much." I stammered a bit. "These visions terrify me. I've got to learn how to control them. I want to use my gift to help people, but my problem is…" and she cut me off.

"Oh, cher, I know. You got what we all get before we learn how to control da gift. But we gon' cure dat today. Dat's right, today. Wait here. Ya hungry?" The universal greeting in Louisiana was always an invitation to eat. No matter what time of day or type of occasion.

Ma-ma and I answered at the same time, "No, thank you."

"Ok. Jus' wait a minute." Miss Lorena left the room.

While we waited, Ma-ma and I looked around the warm, colorful room. It was like nothing I had ever seen. In its own way, it had charm and beauty. The worn, freckled wood floors peeked out from under layers of handwoven wool rugs in a variety of faded colors. We sat in one of the French-inspired settees that lined the walls. The chairs were upholstered in pink and gold brocade fabrics, and two wingback chairs were positioned across from each of them. A coffee table of marble inlay held whatnots of marginal interest. But the true beauty was the display of candles and photos on both her buffet and bookshelves. The buffet was nearly covered in candles that had been burned at a variety of heights. Their sweet, earthy fragrances were sensual nose-play. The candles were flanked by incense and powders in small ceramic dishes and statuary. Photos of men, women, and children were displayed on the bookshelves, each with candles and cards next to them with what I assumed were prayers for their souls. Over-embellished lamps with shades covered in fabrics tinted the room a faint lavender. A floor lamp in the corner of the room glowed with a bright-red light bulb. The connecting dining room sported the familiar reproduction Duncan Phyfe dining table and six chairs, a common set in local homes of the elderly. The seat cushions were in a traditional burgundy, but not so traditional were the snake skins draped across the backs of each chair. I had no idea what that stood for, and I didn't want to know. The room was interesting, if perhaps overstimulating. It could almost pass for a voodoo museum. Closer investigation of the book shelves revealed gris-gris dolls, some with pins and small knives in various parts of their bodies. One doll even had fake blood dripping from its head. Evidently, Miss Lorena was not a pushover. Ma-ma looked at me and motioned her chin toward the gris-gris dolls, stretching her already large eyes. I didn't dare laugh.

The sound of Miss Lorena's slippers scraping against the floors announced her return to the room. "Ok, Ti-Sarah. Let's talk, cher. We have work to do, yeah." Miss Lorena pulled a wingback chair closer to me and Ma-ma. "Now. Ya need ya spiritual channels opened so dat ya always have a pathway to truth. We will do dat with a spirit bath. Now, after dat, we will increase ya spirit gifts to make dem more potent. Dis can only be done wit dem dat's got da gift, so it won't hurt Bernice none to be in da rum. After we do dat, I gon' give you a few tings to take home to help ya stay strong in da gifts. You will need a spirit bath from time to time and to keep these spells for down da road. Ya understand, cher?"

I hesitated for a few seconds to make sure my mind had waded through Miss Lorena's accent with clear understanding and then answered, "Yes, ma'am." I never used that term, but I seemed to be falling under some kind of spell.

"Bien, cher. Now let's go to da bath." Miss Lorena led the way. Turns out, when she had left the room earlier, she had prepared the water and oils for the bath. A light steam and fragrance roamed through the tiny bathroom.

"Dis bath is goat's milk, lavender, parsley, sea salt, and rosemary. Take off your clothes, Ti-Sarah, and soak while me and ya mama recite da spell, cher." Miss Lorena was no longer smiling. Her face held a serious look. As she left the room, I reluctantly undressed and entered the large, claw-footed tub. It was warm and the water creamy with herbs and lavender. It felt soft. I listened to Ma-ma and Miss Lorena while I soaked.

"Now, Catin. Oh, I mean Bernice. I called you Catin. I see Catin's spirit in da rum wit us, yeah Bernice. Here's da spell; we say it slowly five times as Sarah soaks in da bath. Sink deeper into the water, Ti-Sarah. Let's start: Spirit of all dat we shall see, all dat has come, and all dat will be. I am da door. I am da key. I am da light, and I am free. Let da truth be seen in me."

Ma-ma and Miss Lorena slowly recited the spell five times as I closed my eyes. Somehow the words of the spell and the fragrance of the herbal spirit bath combined took my thoughts away. My only focus was on their chant. I began to hum along with them and was lost in the moment. When they stopped, I yawned deeply and felt sleepy. Miss Lorena brought me warmed, fluffy towels to leave the bath. She also brought a colorful caftan for me to wear. I pulled it over my head.

"And now, cher. We reinforce ya power."

Miss Lorena took out a pipe and, I swear, some of the best weed I had ever smelled in my entire Berkeley life. I had to hold back the urge to laugh as she lit up the pipe. Miss Lorena got us stoned as she chanted and hummed about the power of spirit and the power of Sarah. Ma-ma and I got caught up in the moment, buzzed by the weed. Miss Lorena then started to dance around her house while she chanted. She started lighting all of the candles in her place. There must have been about thirty of them and she lit every one of them.

"Um...um. Da power of Sarah is at hand. Da power of Sarah is stronger than any man. Da power of Sarah will work for good. Da power of Sarah will work for good. Um, ya-yah-yah-yah-yah, good!" Miss Lorena continued to dance, repeating her chant.

Ma-ma and I sat on the floor, high and smiling. I don't think my sheltered mother realized we had just smoked marijuana, so I didn't want to ruin the experience by telling her. But I hoped Miss Lorena wasn't going to suggest I take the weed home with me considering airline security and all. I changed back into my clothes as we neared the end of the experience.

Slightly out of breath, Miss Lorena went to her room and returned with a small box of items for me. "Here, cher. Now, dis is a list of tings for ya spirit bath. I know you can't take dat on da plane, but you can buy dem when you get home. Now, here are candles dat will support ya power. I made them, so dey better dan what's in da store. And dis is a special soap and some small gris-gris dolls if anyone ever tryin' to hurt you, cher. Don' take no shit off dem, no. Ya make a doll and put dem in dey place. Make dem sick, yeah." Miss Lorena's eyes sparkled with intention.

"Thank you so much, Miss Lorena. I can't thank you enough. How much do we owe you for this amazing session?" I asked.

"Mais, cher, dis was for Catin. Her spirit asked me to do dis long before ya mama called. And remember, as time passes, ya will become more and more powerful. Ya be able to make ya own spells and dolls and everyting, cher. Ya will carry our tradition. Ya be blessed, cher." Ma-ma and I gathered our things and moved toward the door.

"Miss Lorena, this has been such a blessing. I know Catin was in the room." Ma-ma hugged her. I knew that if my mother was showing any outward signs of affection, she was still buzzed. We walked to the car, waved, and left. As we found our way back to the main highway, Ma-ma didn't realize she was experiencing the classic munchies.

"Sarah, I am starving," she said.

I smiled to myself. "Me too, Ma-ma. Let's find a restaurant."

Somehow my senses seemed heightened, either by the great weed or the magic of Miss Lorena, and I enjoyed every herb and spice of our of dinner. Ironically, Ma-ma and I didn't talk about Miss Lorena and the spiritual adventure, not at dinner, not that night at the hotel, and not on the plane returning to California. In fact, we never mentioned that journey. It became a secret rite between the two of us, held dear and never to be shared with anyone else. Ma-ma knew the ritual with Miss Lorena had changed my life forever, but she never took credit for it, ever.

I test drove my new power on the plane as Ma-ma slept. I recited to myself three times, "All I need to see and know appear to me in this moment of flow." After I quietly repeated the chant I received a head-slapping vision. Vivid, psychedelic colors whirled and sprayed into a mind movie. I saw men in suits dragging Jorge who was in his orange jail jumpsuit. He was screaming but they continued dragging him. They were all in black and I could only see the backs of their heads. The scene was overcome with smoke. The thought came to me that the black suits represented positions of power and the dragging symbolized the frame up. I remained awake all the way back to California, and with stronger determination to find out why Jorge was being framed and who was behind it all.

CHAPTER SIX

O nce back at home, I was audience to an intense dream that night. In it, Miss Lorena danced and smoked her killer weed while Mama and I chanted. A photo of Yadira was perched in the center of the room, flanked by candles and incense. I held a gris-gris doll with Yadira's enlarged eyes and pushed a long stick pin into its stomach as blood gushed out of it. As the doll screamed, I woke up, scared and sweaty. I looked around my room and wondered why I wanted to hurt Yadira. The answer came to me quickly: it was because she wanted to hurt me. I used the weekend to write down everything I learned from Miss Lorena and to go out and buy my supplies. I resolved to make this gift work for me and Manuel.

The next morning was the start of a new week and I called Jean to get organized before going to the office.

"Hi, Jean. How's the office? Still standing?"

"Yes, we haven't been burned down yet." Jean laughed. "By the way; God save us from that Yadira. She is constantly emailing me and the guys for files and updates. I know she's worried but she is a bit much." Jean complained.

"I know it's awkward for you, but please try to keep her in the dark. Tell her we'll do our updates in the meetings and we don't want to pass incomplete files. I don't trust her, so let's be cautious." I said.

"Agreed. And you have had several calls from your investigation team last week. They said it was urgent. I hope you're not mad that I didn't interrupt your trip to tell you that. I figured you didn't want to be disturbed." I could hear the smile in Jean's voice as she referred to Corwin and Caswell as my investigation team. In my mind they had become like a knock-off of the duo from novelist John Steinbeck's book, *Of Mice and Men*, the journey of two migrant workers chasing their dreams: one intelligent but uneducated, the other intellectually challenged.

"You did the right thing. Call them back and try to set up a meeting in the office over lunch. I feel I've lost some time and I may as well jump right back into routine," I said.

"I'm sure they'll be available; they were eager, but I'll send you an e-mail to confirm after I get in touch with them," Jean said.

After going over a few more messages, Jean and I finished up.

"I'll be in a bit late, closer to the lunch meeting. See you then," I said.

"OK," Jean answered, and within the hour, she sent an e-mail with lunch meeting details. I showered and dressed in a blur. I made it to my office and Jean greeted me with a coffee mug filled with our machine-created latte as her eyes rolled toward our conference room and my team. I was certain Caswell was being paid by Manuel, but he ate as if every meal would be his last.

"Heya, Doc Sarah. By the way, can I call you Doc Sarah? I like that better than that long last name of yours." I could see Caswell pile a roast beef, basil, and tomato sandwich into his mouth, not bothering to close it for chewing. Mangled sandwich appeared between each of his words, churning the coffee in my stomach. "And thanks for the fancy grub. I don't get this kinda food much." Caswell smacked his lips.

Corwin did. Despite being a sociopath with limited skills, Corwin enjoyed the good life gifting himself with things such as tailored suits, champagne and fine dining from his family money. The death of his uncle moved him to double-digit millions, he told me one day. His wife had recently left him without wanting anything, which allowed him to enjoy his wealth free of community property. Corwin treated himself to life's pleasures and treasures; his void was companionship and purpose. I had inadvertently helped him with both of those by making him part of the team.

"These sandwiches are good, Sarah. I think I will call you Sarah, since we're peers now." Corwin looked for a reaction from me. I ignored the remark. "Well, anyway, we have important news for you. I wish you would have called us while you were traveling, but here we are now." From Corwin's chastising tone, a stranger would have assumed he was in charge of the meeting and my boss.

"Well, I wasn't available. That is that. So, what's the news?" I had grown impatient with Corwin's new confidence. He nodded for Caswell to begin. Caswell rolled his eyes to the ceiling and pulled a small notepad from his inner coat pocket. "You see, Doc Sarah, once I brought Corwin here up to date on the situation, he started following Yadira immediately. I went along to make him familiar with police surveillance tactics and to show him how to use the listening equipment." Caswell breathed in deeply to accentuate his knowledge and authority. "In addition to that, I've been working my sources, so we have a lot to share. We'll get right to it."

"That's right." Corwin smiled.

"The first and most shocking thing in following Yadira is that we caught her in a lip lock with one of the jailers. Not just once, but several times and a few overnight visits, to say the least." Caswell raised his eyebrows twice, suggesting a sexual liaison.

"That's right." Corwin smiled.

"What? You mean a jailer from…?" I asked.

Caswell cut in, "Yes. A jailer from the same jail of her stepson and the murder. You got it!"

"Holy shit." I was nearly speechless.

"And stay tuned, because it gets better. So I hit up my contacts to get more info. It took a while for one of them to come totally clean on this, and we'll have to get our own proof, of course. When it comes to Timothy, the kid bunking with young Jorge, I got it confirmed that he wasn't your regular inmate; he was a snitch, just like Jorge told you. But get this; there's something about a drug ring that might involve some insiders from either the jail, some high level types and dirty cops. I only got bits and pieces at this point." Caswell cleared his sinuses with a deep, nose-rattling sniff.

I muffled a gag in reaction to Caswell's poor table manners. "So maybe Jorge's cell mate was helping to bust some insiders and turns up dead? Not surprising. I wonder if he told Jorge about the drug ring. When Manuel and I met with Jorge, it was obvious he was hiding some information out of fear. This might be why he's being framed. But what is Yadira's part in this? I'd bet good money Manuel doesn't know that she has that jailer contact, lover, or whatever he is; right?" I asked. I didn't share my visions with the team so I kept to myself the fact that I saw Jorge being dragged by VIPs.

Caswell shoved a third sandwich into his mouth and continued to talk. "No, I'm pretty sure Manuel has no clue about Yadira's um, dating the jailer. So we need Corwin here to step up the surveillance on Yadira while I try to get more on the jailer and this drug ring. We thought this was urgent news, and you needed to know it right away. This game is getting to be more complicated, and if she's playing hide the sheets with a dirty jailer where a murder happened, this could get dangerous." Caswell paused.

"That's right." Corwin smiled.

"You ready for this?" Caswell gave a steady glance and an I-used-to-be-a-cop stare straight into my eyes.

"Hell yeah. We all are. In fact, I need to go on surveillance, too. I want to see if I recognize any of them." I confirmed and looked around the room.

"That's right." Corwin smiled.

Jean, who had been taking notes, looked up. Caswell and I leered at Corwin because of his tedious repetition.

"What?" He looked at us, confused, and then stripped a crust of bread away from his sandwich with pinky finger pointed into the air and chewed it, meekly. "Do you have some champagne?" Caswell shook his head, ignored him, and continued with a plan.

"I need to work the few cops who'll talk to me. We need to find out more about Yadira, the ring, and background on this jailer. His name is Damian Lis. I don't know yet how they met. And we need to know who else is involved."

A cold chill forced its way up my spine, and I shivered in fear. The case had become complicated and dangerous, but piqued my sense of determination.

"Jean. Please add research on Lis to the file you're pulling together on Yadira. We don't need to hear your report on her today because now I want you to do a comparison of the paths of their lives. Let's see where they cross and how. Corwin, keep following her, but let me know your next planned trip. I need to go along. And we can try to discreetly get photos of Yadira with Lis. Caswell will keep giving instructions on procedure for this as well as recordings because we'll need those, too."

"I can do that." Corwin saluted.

"And Caswell, we'll wait to hear more from you and your contacts. Let's reconvene here over lunch in a few days. How about we get together Friday to see what we've all been able to pull together?" I asked.

"That works." Jean nodded.

"Great." Corwin smiled eagerly.

"Check." Caswell folded the sandwich wrappers and cleaned the area in front of him. He returned the notepad to his coat pocket and left. Corwin followed him out.

"I hate to say it, I thought this would be a disaster, but I think this bizarre team actually works," Jean admitted.

I chuckled under my breath. "I know. Truthfully, I thought it would be a disaster in the making, too. But I think we're on to something." We left the conference room for our respective work areas. Jean took her spot at reception, and I sank into the soft leather of my office chair. I had more than a week's worth of neglected mail to scan over. One envelope stood out above the rest. Numbers were obvious in the upper left corner. I could tell that it was prison or jail mail. I knew without opening it that it was from Michael. It was as if something sharp pricked the inside of my stomach. I used my letter opener to slice the envelope top open. My breath was short as I read the brief note. It read: *Sarah, I really need to see you. I know that I'm the last person you'd want to see, but I have to talk to you. Please visit me. Michael.*

I closed my eyes. Vivid colors appeared inside my eyelids. I softly recited, "Show me all I need to know. What does Michael have for me? Should I even go?" A knife-sharp pain pierced my forehead. I opened my eyes, but the pain only deepened. Nausea caused a bitter liquid to fill my mouth, and I saw Michael. He was sitting across from me in the prison visiting area. He appeared robotic, emotionless. He mouthed the words, "I will be of use to you. I will be of use to you." The vision faded. Now, more than once, I had asked for a vision and it appeared. I had a new sense of power over my psychic intuitive gift.

I called out. "Jean. Please get Nikeba on the phone." Seconds later, Jean answered back. "She didn't answer; her office says she's in court, but I left a message."

"Thanks, Jean. I'll try again later. I'll keep playing catch up with these emails." I said.

"And I'll keep trying to pry records from these government offices so we can find out more about Yadira and Lis," Jean answered.

I yelled "Good idea" to Jean, but my mind was really on Michael and why he had been insisting upon seeing me. He almost seemed desperate.

Nikeba won't be happy with me, but she has to help me arrange a prison visit with Michael, quickly.

CHAPTER SEVEN

My life events had the workings of either a great sitcom or a cheap thriller. I returned home with the need for liquid courage. I poured a tall cabernet, pulled index cards from my kitchen recipe drawer, and began to construct the elements of the case on my dining room floor. I needed more visual aids to help trigger my mind and spirit with the case. My crime index cards happened to be labeled "From the Kitchen of Sarah," because I often shared vegetarian and Creole-inspired recipes. They had to do. I constructed card categories, events, places, characteristics, and personas. I lined them up with people and tried to see if connections formed. The phone rang with the personality of Ma-ma and interrupted my rhythm.

"Hello, Sarah. I left a message earlier to let you know that Stacy is here. She was supposed to wait a few weeks but told me she had to get away, so she took a flight and got in today. Your brother Lyle picked her up at the airport. Good thing she didn't try this a few days ago, or we would've been in Louisiana." Ma-ma rambled until she made way back to her accusatory tone of voice. "I wish you would have called me back."

"I had an urgent meeting going on today, Ma-ma. I've been pretty swamped with this case. Remember, we have a young man's life hinging on our work. It's serious." I thought I'd launch a few guilt bombs myself for a change.

"I realize that, but Stacy is family. And I hope that you'll plan to include her socially with you and your friends. She needs to get out so she can forget about her troubles," Ma-ma ordered. It were as if she said, "Remember to invite Stacy to play with your friends." But this wasn't childhood. Stacy was a treacherous, manipulative bitch. I was knee-deep in the beginnings of my first criminal case, and I was emotionally stuck between an unaccepted dinner invitation from Lance, whom I now secretly called Dr. Nerd, and hot flirtations with my former lawyer. I didn't want to make time for Stacy and her inevitable bullshit.

But, Ma-ma was persistent. "I'm sure you'll work it out." She slammed the phone down.

I couldn't help but resent that Ma-ma wasn't as committed to my recovery from heartbreak last year, but that was no surprise. Stacy was more the daughter she wanted, and I was more the daughter she got. Stacy even looked more like Ma-ma than I did. She had the same olive-toned skin; silky, black, wavy hair; straight nose; and figure-eight curved body style. Of that list, all I had were the curves. My caramel-colored skin was nearly a perfect match to the color of my hair and eyes, a bizarre human monochrome. I was often called an odd-cute. People assumed I was biracial, the product of a blond man and a black woman. But those familiar with Louisiana's Creole culture knew that centuries of race mixing was outed in the vast array of skin hues, hair textures, and eye colors. I could feel the heat on the back of my neck as I became pissed off at Ma-ma's over-the-top concern for Stacy and her attempt to pressure me to put my responsibilities on hold.

"I've been busy rebuilding my life, but sure, I'll put my future on hold for Stacy," I said sarcastically to no one.

I returned to the floor and my crime kitchen recipe cards. I had cards for Yadira, Jorge, his deceased cellmate Timothy Reston, and now a new card for jailer Damian Lis. The problem was there was too much blank space on my cards, too much information lacking to make any of it tell a complete story and point to a murderer. I was ready to see Michael and to see if he had information to fill in some of the blanks, as my vision suggested. I had to bug Nikeba, so I called her at home and told her what I wanted.

"Jesus! Are you crazy, Sarah? Do we have to relive last year's drama?" Nikeba was full on irritated.

"Just set up the meeting. I take full responsibility for whatever happens after that. You don't understand, I am guided to do this meeting," I pleaded.

"Here you go with the potions, notions, and spells. But I hate to admit it, when all is said and done, you're spot on accurate. But, I hope you know what you're doing this time. I'll ask my husband, and we'll get the visit to San Quentin arranged. Crazy-assed lady. Love you, bye," Nikeba said.

"Thank you. Thank you, Nikeba. And thank Steve. Love you both!" We hung up.

Knowing I would face Michael again led me to brush aside my crime kitchen recipe cards and finish off my bottle of wine. I ended the night distracted, un-watching a few movies and nibbling small amounts of cheese. I was anxious about the upcoming meeting with my former fake fiancé. I hadn't seen him in nearly a year. I wondered; what will he look like? Why is he so determined for me to visit him and what could he possibly know? *What the hell will this be like?*

The morning rushed in and I struggled with the my office door knob while I carried supplies we couldn't live without; a box of my crime kitchen recipe cards, a tray of two large lattes, and a bottle of Kettle One vodka for those tough days we could only end with a shot. Jean heard my struggle and opened the door. I nearly lost balance in my four-and-a-half-inch Rene Caovilla booties.

"That sounds like a great idea." Jean perked up over the idea of the cards. "I like the crime cards and the pictures you're drawing, too. When we put all of these with the files and notes, I think we'll make a lot of progress, Dr. Sarah." Jean smiled while I taped the cards to a white board. Organization always appealed to Jean.

"Yeah, this is some pretty cool work that we do now." I stood back, admiring my configuration. We spent the next few hours dissecting the information we had so far. We worked and reworked pieces and hypotheses until we both tired of it. "Let's take a break," I suggested.

"Yeah, the mail is here and I need to open it." Jean went to her desk.

My mobile phone buzzed. "And I have a text from Nikeba. Interesting. Thanks to Steve's connections, my visit to San Quentin is set up for the next week."

"Oh, wow." Was all that Jean had to say. She hated Michael for all he had put me through and she never had much to say when his name came up. I didn't try to force her to talk about him.

I would see Michael for the first time since his murder trial. This time, I didn't fear him. I was curious about his mental state and health, but my mind was on Jorge's case and how Michael could help me free the young man.

Jean yelled. "Whoa!"

"What's wrong?" I called out.

"Dr. Sarah, I just found something you'll want to know." Jean walked into my office holding a large envelope and documents close to her chest.

"What? What's wrong? What's that?"

"I was opening the mail and got this." Jean handed the envelope and its contents to me.

"Read the first piece of paper," she said. I scanned the document and had never been more caught off guard in my life. I couldn't find words. "Holy shit. This is unbelievable, Jean. This is…I don't know what to say."

"Can you believe it?" Jean asked.

"No. I can't believe it. If I didn't see it, I wouldn't believe it."

Jean had managed to get the birth certificate of Timothy Reston, Jorge's murdered cellmate. It read: *Father unknown. Mother, Yadira Anda.* Anda was Yadira's maiden name before she married high school teacher Daniel Lopez and became stepmother to his son, Jorge. The year of the birth meant she had the boy when she was in undergraduate school at Cal State East Bay and maybe put him up for adoption. Jean and I were in shock. "Wow. Wow. Wow." I was repeating myself now like Corwin.

"Shocking. Shocking." Jean kept saying, as she looked at the vital statistics record shaking her head.

"Shocking? I can't process this. I'm stunned." I fell back into my chair. "Now, we have to get more details like whether she knew that Timothy was her son; did he grow up around her, who the hell the father was or is…or is this Damian the father…I mean there's so much that this could mean." I was rambling. "Oh my God, Manuel really doesn't know this woman at all. Or did he know this stuff and choose not to share it with me?"

"Well, at some point, you have to put it in front of him; right?" Jean nervously bit her top lip.

I nodded. "Yeah, but will he hate me for it or appreciate it?"

"Yeah, that could go either way," She added.

"Well, first, let's get the guys here. Tell them they have to clear their schedules and get here today for an emergency meeting. Get them lunch—they love that, you know. Then, schedule a meeting with Manuel for next week. I'm sure he's expecting an update, and we don't want him to think we're not making progress." My eyes were fixed on my office wall, but not focused. I was still numb.

"Ok. I'm on it." Jean went back to her desk.

I kept staring at the papers, thinking I needed to know Yadira's story beyond what anyone could tell me. I quietly called upon my gift. "All that I need to know and see, come and show yourself to me. Yadira Lopez is a mystery; bring her spirit and truths to me." I repeated the words with my eyes closed, three times. My head was spinning, and my stomach churned. The foul taste of bitter acid lined my tongue. I saw a young Yadira at a hospital in labor. I saw the hands of a man next to her, holding her hand. He shook his head, as if with regret, and then left. He was an older man. He kissed her cheek, and he walked out before she delivered. She cried and howled in pain. She had the baby alone. The vision vanished. Yadira seemed to have been abandoned by the father, an older man. I assumed she put Timothy up for adoption.

Jean called out, "I have the guys on board, but not for today; tomorrow for lunch. They want to bring more info, too.

"Ok. That works," I yelled back.

In preparation for the meeting, I poured through a growing pile of folders and documents. Old newspaper articles, files from UCLA, Cal State East Bay, and even a high school newspaper article were in Jean's extensive files. The school newspaper article highlighted a young Yadira for receiving a four-year scholarship to Cal State East Bay. It was clear from the story that she was from a working class family, and college would not have been possible without the scholarship. While I worked to create my own document of notes from the files, I noticed an e-mail notice pop up from Jean. She had sent me meeting details with Manuel, confirmed by his office. I would work in that office that morning and go over updates with him. Little did he know, the updates would blow his mind and I wanted to include the entire team.

"Holy mother of God!" Caswell sat at the head table in my office conference room and was nearly knocked out of the chair by the news about Yadira and the fact that she was the actual birth mother of Timothy Reston, the deceased cellmate of her stepson, Jorge. "Were you able to get any info on the father?" he asked once he was able to settle with the information.

"Not yet. We think he may have been an older man, but we have to do more digging," I said.

"And I will bet you a paycheck this will tie in to the murder of this kid, too," Caswell insisted.

"This is getting good." Corwin was inappropriately excited. The rest of us were still stunned.

Before the team dug into Jean's research and my crime kitchen recipe cards, Caswell and Corwin had headlines of their own to share.

"As you can imagine, my contacts inside the PD are tight-lipped about the drug ring and who is involved. They confirmed it, but they wouldn't tell me who is part of it, they would only say the names would blow my mind. And Corwin now had his first photos of Yadira meeting with some of those contacts.

"Unfortunately, I only have the backs of their heads. My hiding place wasn't at a great angle. It was a parking garage so I had to be careful." Corwin was apologetic.

"That's OK. I'll be there next time to help." I looked over the pictures and was reminded of my vision while flying back from Louisiana. The backs of heads of powerful people, dragging Jorge. I was proud of the initial work of my low rent posse of an investigative team, they had hit it out of the park.

"Doc Sarah, we need to take this to Manuel. We can't keep him in the dark too much longer." Caswell scratched his head.

"That's exactly what I was thinking. I have a meeting scheduled with him; let's make it a group update," I agreed. "But we have to make sure we have enough to impress him. I have a feeling this will hit him hard, because he's known Yadira since law school, and we don't want him to jump into denial because our evidence is too flimsy. He thinks a lot of Yadira. Tearing her down might cause him to turn on us," I added. "Corwin, let me know when you will be following Yadira again and I will come along. We'll try our best to get faces. Two cameras might be better than one." I said.

We all agreed to keep digging with the goal of filling in the Yadira story to update Manuel. It was a story that was beginning to unfold. As three separate conversations hummed around the conference room, Jean left the room to answer the phone at her desk in the reception area. She returned and tapped me on the shoulder. "Dr. Sarah, it's your mother. She says it's urgent."

"Oh. OK. Excuse me, you guys." I went into my office to take the call.

"Sarah, meet me at Alta Bates right away. It's Stacy. I have to follow the ambulance to the hospital." Ma-ma was out of breath.

"What? Ambulance—what happened?"

"Just get over there. Now!" She hung up.

I flew past the others, yelling, "Family emergency!" My heart raced because despite Stacy being my miserable adversary, she was still family; and in the Creole culture, the shackles of that obligation are never loosened. I ran to find out what trouble my albatross had gotten into and what trouble she would likely cause.

CHAPTER EIGHT

Sitting in the waiting room of Alta Bates hospital in Berkeley took me back to sitting in a Louisiana hospital and the death of my mentor, Aunt Cat. This time her daughter was the patient. Ma-ma had found her newly arrived houseguest, Stacy, on the bedroom floor. She had swallowed a handful of sleeping pills. She would survive. There's an expression about the long life of sinister people; something about heaven not wanting them and the devil not quite being ready. According to that adage, Stacy would be with us for an eternity.

Ma-ma sat next to me shaking her head in disbelief. "I knew she was depressed, but to try to kill herself?"

"I don't think she really wanted to kill herself, Ma-ma. She left half of the pills in the bottle." It was a ploy as far as I was concerned. Stacy did everything for a reason, and I was sure that this was no exception. Her real motive would reveal itself soon enough.

"You just stop that. Stacy is in a deep depression. You would think a therapist would understand that. And anyway, she needs you to help her find her footing in a new life!" Ma-ma was gearing up for a "play nice" lecture.

I knew this would come around to being my fault. And what the hell is 'footing?'

"I ask you to do one small thing. To take a little time from your fancy days to help your cousin. Catin would be hurt to know you don't want to be of aid to her daughter in her time of need. Is that too much of an inconvenience? Are you too busy to help someone who is down on their luck? Did I raise you to be *that* selfish?" Ma-ma was on a self-righteous, preachy roll.

"No. You're right. I'll help. As soon as she's well." I caved because I knew there was no reasoning with the unreasonable.

Whatever.

And before I could offer more empty words, a familiar smile, hosted by a white lab coat and wobbly legs, walked in our direction. My last year's crush and ungraceful one-night stand, Dr. Lance Gaston, noticed us in the hallway and walked awkwardly toward us. For weeks I had crushed on Lance when he would come into Marlin's on the Bay to hear me sing. Lance was what Creole's called, high yellow with straight hair. He had an unusually small nose, pretty dark eyes and an athletic build. He was one of those guys who seemed cool until he opened his mouth. Lance took nerd to new levels; he had a corny sense of humor, a hissing laugh and spoke like an encyclopedia. *It's a sacrilege for a gorgeous man to be as dull as unseasoned rice.* I hadn't made time to take Lance up on his dinner invitation because I dove head first into Manuel's case. Admittedly, I couldn't seem to hold the same level of excitement or interest in Lance after drunken, spontaneous sex caused him to avoid me for weeks. But in the end, he was a friend. I owed him my life for his help in Michael's murder trial fiasco. Lance was still a handsome and smart man to me, but something wasn't quite there.

"Hello, Mrs. Jean-Louis, Sarah." Lance nodded to Ma-ma first and then to me. "I thought it was the two of you. What are you doing here? Who is sick?" The center of his eyebrows spiked with curiosity. I noticed he still refused to use contractions; even in every day conversation.

"Hello, Dr. Gaston. It's so good to see you." Ma-ma smiled in the way she only smiled when eligible bachelors were within a certain radius of me. "How have you been? We miss seeing you and are so grateful for the way you helped Sarah last year." For a moment, she seemed to had forgotten all about Stacy. Ma-ma was now on the hunt for a husband for me, and God knows, a doctor would be perfect in her mind. Lance was a strikingly handsome guy. I don't know who recommended he trade in his inch-thick glasses for contacts, but it helped. His glasses had magnified parts of his face or anything caught in their trajectory. Lance had a classic Creole look, which was something Ma-ma also liked about him.

I cleared my throat. "Lance, my cousin Stacy has recently moved to California from Louisiana after a bitter divorce. She's visiting with Ma-ma and, unfortunately took too many sleeping pills." I gave a deadpanned explanation.

"Oh no. I am so sorry. Well, although I am in pediatrics, I can still keep an eye on her for you guys," he offered.

The nurse who tended to Stacy walked out of her room, and the three of us went in to see her. Once inside, Lance seemed to have difficulty closing his mouth. Even after a pumped stomach and wearing little to no makeup, my cousin was a stunning woman. Stacy's almond eyes seemed larger. Her black, wavy hair framed her flawless face, and she had managed to apply fire red lipstick. Stacy displayed fully rounded cleavage because she was not wearing the hospital issue gown but her own lingerie, a peignoir.

While I struggled to hide my disgust, I broke the trance to stomach an introduction. "Lance, this is my cousin Stacy. Stacy, you remember me telling you about Dr. Lance Gaston." She simultaneously pepped up and pushed out her chest.

"Oh, yes." Stacy used a soft-spoken, fake weakened, wispy voice. "It is such a pleasure to meet you. I have heard wonderful things about you." She smiled weakly and stared straight into Lance's eyes.

"Uh, I, uh, let me know if there is anything I can do to help you while you are staying in our facility. I am here every day, and all you need do is to have them page me if you need me." He handed Stacy a business card. I assumed it was dripping with drool. Lance acted as if Stacy were at his hotel and he were a bellman.

Oh, puh-lease. I can't watch this without a vomit pail.

I was more than ready to exit. "All of you are in good hands, and I have to leave, so I'll say good-bye. Stacy, I'm glad you're feeling better. We need to get you out of the house when you are fully recovered. Ma-ma, I'll check in with you later. Lance, good to see you." I waved and left before anyone could respond. It sickened me to see another man fall for Stacy, especially one who, unbeknownst to her, had dumped me the year before. In the honest corners of my mind, I realized that I didn't really want Lance, but I definitely didn't want him to want Stacy. I turned my attention to Yadira and a case that had the potential to become my new obsession. I didn't have an appointment or anywhere I had to be, I just had to leave the hospital and the Stacy show. I went home to fill my mind with my new life because although I didn't really want Lance, his reaction to Stacy hurt—bad. It hurt both my ego and my heart.

I had planted myself on my living-room floor, knee-deep in more crime kitchen recipe cards, placing them together like puzzle pieces as I wiped my tear-stained face. I hated myself for falling victim to Stacy's power to make me feel like the ugly, unlucky cousin again. Even from a hospital bed, with no money and no home, she had bested me. I watched the tears flow onto my cards, blurring my carefully crafted notes.

The ring of my phone startled me.

"Dr. Jean-Louis, it's the front desk. Can Manuel Cabrera come up?"

"Uh, yes…um, yes. Tell him which floor, and yes, let him up." I sniffled. Manuel had never been to my place before. He knew my address, of course, but he had never visited my condo unit. I was caught off guard. I ran to the bathroom to wipe away evidence of my tears and to do a quick makeup touch-up. The doorbell rang within minutes. I opened it, and my stomach did gymnastic flips. The tanned chest of the tall, handsome man was eye level for me. It was framed by a gray shirt, black sports jacket, tight jeans, and perfect Italian leather-laced shoes.

"Hi. Welcome. I'm surprised to see you. Were you in the area, or were you…" I forced a calm voice but was cut off midstream. Manuel grabbed me and kissed me so intensely, all feeling left my legs. It didn't matter, because he was pretty much holding me up.

"Do you have dinner plans? I need to be with you tonight." He spoke softly, and looked directly into my eyes.

I was never cool like the women in the movies. "Yes. I mean, no. No, I don't have plans, so yes, I can do dinner with you. I mean yes, plans with you. So no plans. You know." Thankfully, he kissed me again. I think to shut me up.

"Good," he whispered and chuckled.

"Where?" I asked.

"Follow me." He grabbed my hand. I grabbed my purse and followed.

Eyes around the tiny restaurant settled on Manuel and me, for no other reason than that we were two expensive looking professionals sitting in an authentic dive. It wasn't a chic, trendy spot in the city of Alameda but rather the kind of place people went for real Mexican food like handmade tortillas and generously liquored margaritas. No one spoke English, but they didn't have to. Years of charm school were laid waste while I ate with both hands and slurped my drink.

Manuel laughed at me. "I'm glad you like the food here. Hahaha. Can I get you a shovel?"

My speech was slightly slurred. "OK. Make fun. But it's nice to let go sometimes. And I don't usually drink margaritas, but these are great. I wonder what's different?" I asked.

"They're ninety proof." Manuel laughed. "Before we get too drunk—because we will—I want to tell you about something strange that happened to me."

"What?" I wondered if it was a Yadira-related story.

"Somebody shot at me last night." He was motionless.

"What! Did you call the police? Were you hurt? Oh my God. Why did you wait to tell me this? What the hell?" I ranted. "Did you get a look at the person? Man or woman? Tell me everything that happened?"

"Yes, I called the police and made out a report. No, I wasn't hurt. Sarah, I've been shot at before. I didn't notice anybody behind me while I was driving, but it was evident this guy had been following me for a while. I left the office and pulled out of the garage. I saw a parking space in front of my favorite liquor store on Sansome St. and you know how rare it is to get a parking space like that in the city." Manuel took another bite of his rice and beans.

"Did the shooter jump out at you?" I fought tears.

"When I got out of the car, I noticed a guy in a black suit. He seemed over-dressed for San Francisco and as silly as this sounds, he was wearing a fake beard. Crazy.

"You're kidding." *Another mention of a black suit from my vision.*

"Not at all. The guy had on dark glasses and a fake beard. I thought to myself, bad look dude, and kept walking. The guy brushed past me and something told me to turn around. I saw him pull out a gun, I ducked and ran into the store. That bastard ran off. I called the police but I didn't even see a car so I didn't have license plate information or anything only a goofy description." Manuel bit his bottom lip. He was intense and angry.

"I bet the cops thought you were crazy with the fake beard thing." I gave a brief chuckle.

"Yeah. Standing in a liquor store giving that description didn't help. But in San Francisco, not implausible." Manuel laughed.

"Priceless." I couldn't hold my laughter back. I imagined the officer's faces as Manuel described the perp and it played out hilariously in my mind. I knew we had extended our laughter to relieve the tension of what was actually a murder attempt. Bold and aggressive.

"But it makes me wonder what is really going on in this case. I know you just started, but maybe I shouldn't have involved you in this. That's why I came straight to you without calling ahead. Sorry for that. I needed to be with you and to tell you this one might be more dangerous than I thought. I couldn't live with myself if something happened to you. I can't put you in this position." Manuel's eyes showed deep caring and concern for me. It felt good.

"Sorry, too late, I'm in. All the way in. Listen, listen; you saved my life." I grabbed both of Manuel's hands. "You kept me out of the bad end of Michael's murder trial. You made my weak-assed story believable. I won't leave this case. I'll be careful, but I'm going to find out why...why this Lopez kid is being framed and why someone doesn't want you, or us, to help him. And you sure know how to ruin a good b-b-buzz." I was firm, but I laughed.

Manuel's look was warm and intense. He leaned to kiss me. I met him more than halfway. I lost track of time as we continued to kiss. We smiled and finished our drinks. Manuel's hand had made way under the table, through my skirt, and settled between my thighs. By the time he asked if I wanted to go home with him, my answer seemed predictable. I couldn't believe it, but the moisture between my legs and the tequila in my belly didn't fog my clarity. I whispered, "I can't believe what I'm about to say. I'm incredibly hot for you, but I want to be sure it's not the margaritas causing your attraction to me. I want it to happen when we're not this drunk. I hope you understand." I glanced the owner and his wife, our waitress, smiling as they watched us. I hoped they only saw the kissing and not what was happening under the table.

Manuel smiled and pulled his finger out of my vagina. He kissed me deeply again. "That's my girl; let's go." I stumbled a bit as I got up. I was experiencing tipsy-horny fusion. I was fine with my decision, difficult as it was. He paid the check, and we walked to the car. While outside we kissed, and he drove me home.

I felt compelled to set up the next date once I was out of the car and saying good night. "I hope there will be a next time," I braved.

"I have a feeling there is no end to next times with us, Sarah." Manuel smiled and turned up his music. He drove off.

Once inside my place, I was a mix of horny and dreamy mind-racing thought. Manuel and this case held powerful magnetism for me. No amount of doubt would've turned me away. I was all in. I worked my way out of my clothes and into my lingerie and dropped in place. Once asleep, I dreamed vividly about a large bird circling me like a vulture, toying with me before swooping in for a kill. I spit fire at it, covering it in flames. The bird burned completely, and all I could see were its eyes. Familiar eyes.

Funny how you can wake up embarrassed, all alone. I had fallen asleep on my sofa, too wasted to make it to bed. All I wanted was a fragrant bath, but the phone rang. It was that damned Stacy.

"Hey, couzan. I'm so grateful that you came to see me in the hospital in my time of need, cher. I know how business you are. Well, they released me last night, and I been resting so well." Stacy had a way of using words incorrectly.

"Sarah, I know that I have to pick myself up and begin to live again, not die. My momma would want that for me, you know, cher?" Stacy was one of those women whose verbal skills weren't strong, but she managed to sound seductive even when not trying. Or maybe she was actually always trying.

I faked it. "I understand, Stacy. I want to be helpful to you as you begin your new life."

"Well, mon cher, I been thinking about that, yeah. And I thought, well, Sarah don't have a man so she's probably free for a Sunday brunch. I know how you always talked about your Sunday jazz brunches with your friends. I would like to go to one of them, yeah."

That country cow is still trying to put me down. Sarah don't have a man. If she only knew.

Stacy continued, "So I had an idea, and your Ma-ma thinks it's a great idea. What if we ask that nice Dr. Lance to go with us to a nice brunch this Sunday? That would be easy for me and cheer us both up, you know? I called him, and he said he would like to." She paused.

"So you called Lance first?" I was taken aback.

"I didn't think you would care, cher," Stacy snarled.

"It's just a matter of what's appropriate. Not whether I care or not," I shot back.

"Well, when a man gives me his card and says, 'Call me,' seems appropriate to call him...or did I miss something?" she asked sarcastically.

"You missed a sense of basic courtesy and manners. As in, that's Sarah's friend, maybe I ask Sarah, first. You know, out of respect for Sarah." My voice raised.

"I can't believe how you making so much outta this, cher. I was just trying to set up a fun time. I didn't think you had any claim to Lance. Neither of you gave me that impression. It seems you dated last year, but that's long over. If I have it wrong, correct me. I don't want to cause hard feelings. That's the last thing I want to do. You know." Stacy was artificially contrite.

She had gained ground in manipulating me, so I dialed it back. "You're right. There's nothing between me and Lance. It's just not the way I'm used to doing things, but on second thought, no harm done. What time?" I asked. I was still fuming, but I covered it up.

"Lance said to leave that up to you because you know better where and all that stuff," Stacy said with snide triumph in her voice.

"Let me call my favorite place and see how it'll be for next Sunday. I'll let you know." I quickly hung up and took a few deep, calming breaths. *That button-pushing, uneducated whore!*

Once I got beyond the anger, I called Chico. I refused to let Stacy believe this brunch bothered me. Chico was the piano player at Marlin's on the Bay. It's the place where I sang with him before the trial made me stage-shy.

"Chello?" Chico answered in his fabulous-ness way.

"Hey, girlfriend. How have you been?" I asked.

"I'm working it. I miss you, Ms. Sarah. What's been going on?" he asked.

"The cheat sheet is that now that my family therapy practice is shot, I'm helping with murder investigations, starting with my former lawyer and a case for him. Remember Manuel?"

"Um. Um. You mean mucho guapo? His fine ass should be a moving violation."

I laughed. "Yes, Chico, Manuel is fine. The other big news is that my bitch cousin, Stacy, is here on her ass. Her husband left her, so she moved from Louisiana into Ma-ma's place."

"Whaaaat?"

"Yeah. She's living at Ma-ma's to get on her feet. I think she came here to snag a man. She's run through all the prospects in small town Louisiana. Anyway, she has her eyes on Lance, already. She invited him to a Sunday jazz brunch and wants me to set it up."

"That heifer. Is she serious?" he asked.

"I was pissed at first, but I don't care. I don't really want Lance. He was helpful last year, but I don't really feel anything for him. It just bruises my ego. But, I'll play along. What's happening at the club for jazz brunch Sunday? Do you have any big groups, or is it a good time for us to come?" I asked.

"A great time. It'll be kind of slow for the next few Sundays. We don't have anyone else booked, just me on piano and Junior on bass. You can sing a few songs if you feel like it. Show that witch whose town this is." Chico laughed.

"Yeah, that might be fun, but you know, since the trial, I don't like getting on stage anymore. But we'll plan on eleven thirty. See you then. Love you."

"Love you too, and bring that fine-ass Spanish salsa!" Chico said.

"Stop that. I think I'll wait and roll him out later when I have Stacy good and overconfident. See you Sunday." I hung up.

CHAPTER NINE

The next few days were filled with the monotony of research and paperwork. My Saturday plan was to sit on my couch, binge-watch movies with homemade martinis, and not come out until the Sunday brunch from hell with Stacy and Lance. I figured I deserved a day to myself before that experience, but Saturday turned out to be a pivotal day in the case.

"Hello?" I was tempted to ignore my phone and continue shaking martinis, but I answered, anyway.

"Doc Sarah. Sorry for bothering you on a Saturday, but Corwin's been following Yadira all morning. He said she's headed back to the parking garage where she met up with the black suit guys last time. It's not far from you in downtown Oakland off Broadway. He wants you to meet him at the intersection of Broadway and 14th, then you two can get a hiding place in the garage to take pictures and record them. I set him up with audio surveillance equipment. Can you get over there in a hurry?" Caswell asked.

"Hell, yeah. I'm on my way. Be there in a few minutes." I hung up and put my martinis in the refrigerator for later. I grabbed my purse and camera, rudely blocked the closing elevator door to jump in and go down to my parking garage.

I was in downtown Oakland in about eight minutes. I had timed myself. I pulled up next to Corwin who was easy to spot standing at Broadway and 14th with what looked like a damn towel wrapped around his head. Corwin's protective head gear against evil inspiration on this day was a purple turban fail. The fabric looked more like a bath towel than exotic silk.

Corwin walked over to my passenger side window as I let the window down.

"Yadira is already in that garage across the street. I think you should park out here because it's quieter if we walk in than drive into the garage. I was lying down in this spot while I waited for you so nobody would take it. You can park here." Corwin whispered as he pointed down.

I must be fucking crazy. I'm in a life and death situation with a nut.

"OK. Thanks." I parked and we walked into the parking garage, tiptoeing and looking all around. We found the group meeting far enough away, but close enough for my wide angle camera lens and for Corwin to record.

Corwin tested his audio device and it made a strange beep. I grabbed it.

"Turn that fucking thing off!"

"Uh oh. That wasn't good." Corwin whispered.

I whispered forcefully. "No shit, Sherlock Holmes, what gave you that clue? I'll take the pictures, you try to pick up their conversation." I was frustrated but shook it off. Corwin and I quietly got to work, him recording while I took several photos. We left the garage, unnoticed. I went home to download photos, and Corwin went to meet with Caswell to go over the audio recordings. We agreed to do an early evening team meeting to go over the materials and bring Manuel up to date.

Before five o'clock, I was sitting in my office conference room. Within minutes, Manuel and the rest of the crew had assembled around the mid-sized reclaimed wood conference table in my office. The table was flanked with black Herman Miller executive chairs, the kind made of leather and chrome. The ivory colored conference room walls were adorned with eclectic art; three from Ghanaian artist Vin Azor, a few from emerging American artists and two reproductions of post-impressionist, Gauguin. I had asked Jean to call them all together for an emergency meeting to view the photos I had downloaded and printed, to listen to Corwin's audio recordings. This was Manuel's first time meeting with the team. Caswell led the meeting.

"I'll place the recorder in the middle of the table so you can all hear," Caswell said. Manuel looked perplexed but paid close attention.

I explained, "Manuel, Caswell has trained Corwin in surveillance so that someone inconspicuous could help us gather photos and information. I went along earlier today and we hit big. We've been working for a few weeks, following Yadira and others, and have critical information to share," I added.

Manuel looked at me, confused and mouthed the word, "What?" I nodded and mouthed, "It's OK."

Caswell began. "Everyone, this case has taken a serious and scandalous turn. Thanks to Doc Sarah and Corwin here, we now have strong evidence and we'll need to move fast in some way. Here's what we know so far." Corwin nodded in acknowledgment of his role, he had changed head gear. He tipped his wide-brimmed straw hat tied with yellow ribbon. Caswell spread files and photos across the table as he spoke.

"I think we're all on the same page that young Jorge is being framed for the murder of cellmate Timothy Reston. Well, after some surveillance, we have learned the following things." Caswell turned to Manuel. "Manuel, you might wanna hold on to your seat." He continued. "Thanks to the great work of one Corwin, we know that Yadira and jailer Damian Lis seem to be more than friends, if you get my drift." Caswell was doing his now-famous circular motion with his right hand. Manuel looked at Caswell and then looked at me, eyes stretched with surprise.

Manuel interrupted, "She's sleeping with the jailer?"

"Yes, Manuel. And we have compromising photos. Let him continue. There's more you'll want to know." I attempted to quiet him. I showed him the photos of Damian, a tall, blond, muscular man with a square jaw and piercing blue eyes.

"Seriously?" His voice went up an octave.

"Yes, but please. You want to hear this." I put my hand over his.

"OK." He nodded.

"And thanks to the fine research of one Jean, we also have now discovered that Yadira is the biological mother of the now-deceased Timothy Reston. She put him up for adoption right after the birth, and we don't know if she even knows he's the same kid," Caswell continued.

Manuel stood up and slammed his chair into the table. "What? The dead kid was her son? Good God! Did she know this and keep this from me, and I'm trying to help her ass?" Manuel pounded the table. He was overwhelmed by the information. I wondered if we should have told him earlier, but I knew he would require proof. And as if he read my mind, Manuel reached for the photos and files. He reviewed them as Caswell went on with the update. *As sure as I'm a Jean-Louis, this man had a thing with Yadira. He is way too emotional. I don't think I believe they were never involved.*

"What you will hear on this recording and see in Sarah's photos, is a meeting of Yadira, who is in the black leather jacket, Lis, two cops, an unidentified guy, with well-known criminal judge Phillip Ackers."

"Fucking Ackers," Manuel said under his breath.

"You'll hear them talking about the drug ring that my contacts had told me about. This case seems to be centered around this ring." Caswell pressed the start button to begin playing the recording, and we all leaned in to listen. It was apparent the recording began in the middle of a conversation:

"Well, all of you make sure my name is not connected to any of this shit, that's all."

"That's Ackers." Manuel spoke up. "I know his voice." Corwin nodded in agreement.

"Judge, we've managed to keep you clean all this time. We won't screw up now."

"And that's Damian the jailer." Corwin explained.

"Yeah, that's good and fine, Damian, but now you have a murder to handle. I was in for the money, but I sure as hell didn't want this level of escalation. What the fuck were you guys thinking and how the hell did all of this happen? Who really killed the kid? On second thought, I don't want to know. I don't care." Ackers' voice spiraled.

Yadira spoke up. "My stepson has been charged with the murder. He was the cellmate of the guy, who was a well-known snitch."

"Oh, that's fucking great. A jailhouse, connected snitch bunked up with your step kid, sharing a space, likely talked his goddamn head off. Now he turns up dead, and you believe someone won't connect that to you and us? What kind of fucked-up lawyer are you? And whatever hare-brained strategy this was supposed to be has just put all of us at risk. This operation now has lines to all of us. You fucking idiots!" Ackers yelled.

"No, you see, judge, when we found out that Timothy maybe knew about us, we wanted to make sure neither of them could do anything," Yadira pleaded, but he cut her off.

"Yeah. So you had him killed? How is that working? Don't answer. You don't have an answer. Damian, get your shit together. Fix this. All of you. Fix this or I will." Judge Ackers launched the threat as he walked away.

Yadira spoke again. "Why didn't you guys speak up? I never was in agreement with putting the snitch guy in with Jorge. Damian, that never made sense to me, but I deferred to your plan. Despite that, we have our police officers who've managed to get themselves assigned to the murder investigation. I have my law partner defending Jorge so I can suppress any evidence I would need to so he loses the case. The only problem is, he brought in that crazy so-called, psychic woman who was in that scandal last year. I got a bad feeling about her. We really don't need that bitch snooping around. But I believe we can scare her off or discredit her. I'm trying to make sure Manuel loses this case and doesn't find out about our operation. So is it too much to ask for you guys to stand up for me? Especially you, Damian! You let me take all of the heat from the judge." Yadira's voice was filled with frustration.

"Babe. You know that when the judge is that pissed, it doesn't do any good to try to talk to him. We got this. Go home. Relax. We'll make sure Jorge doesn't talk. The other jailers have him too scared to take a piss. And we have all of the drug shipments on hold until we get past this murder. It's handled. Ackers is nervous that's all," Damian said.

"OK. Call me later," she had a disgusted tone. The sound of her heels striking the pavement signaled that she had left.

"Are you worried about her?" The unidentified man spoke to Damian.

"No, I can handle her. Let's get out of here," Damian said to the others. Then there was silence. Caswell turned off the recording.

All eyes fell on me. Manuel's eyes had turned into tight slits of burning anger. I pointed to the photos. I stood to explain each photo. "These are the pictures with the judge. Here are the two cops. We never heard their names. This is the unidentified man in dark glasses. No one ever used his name, either. And you see Yadira and Damian here at the meeting, and here are Corwin's earlier photos of them kissing on a different day." I sat back down.

Manuel spewed scary anger. "That bitch. That deceptive, lying, sneaky, crooked bitch. I have opened up my practice and the firm to her. This could have ramifications to our firm, the partners—I mean, this is a can of worms. I have to think of how I want to handle this." Manuel ran his right hand through his hair. He looked around the room, his dark eyes seemingly in flames. "Thank goodness we won't have that punk, Judge Ackers on the bench in this case, because we've already been assigned a court room, but this needs a strategy." As the words left his mouth, a shrill sound reminiscent of the Fourth of July broke loudly, and a sharp object shot through the conference room window and into my Gauguin. It was a bullet. Within seconds, we had all dropped to the floor, except for Caswell, who reached into his coat and brandished what I later learned was a Glock, or as some call it, serious shit. He crawled combat style, leading with his elbows around the floor, and peered out of the window, prepared to shoot to kill. We heard a car speed off. We waited a few minutes until all was quiet and crawled into the windowless reception area. Caswell brought the files, photos, and recordings into that area.

"Strike two," Manuel announced. We all stood up and took seats.

"What do you mean, strike two?" Caswell asked.

"I was shot at in front of a liquor store in the city a few days ago. All I could see was a tall guy in a dark suit with a fake beard and dark glasses. In fact, let me look over these photos again at the guy in the dark glasses." Manuel motioned to Caswell for the pictures. He handed the pictures to Manuel. "About this getting shot at; don't you think you shoulda, oughtta tell me those things?" Caswell asked.

"I'm sorry, but since I didn't know about all of this information, I didn't realize all of the underlying issues in this case. Maybe all of you shoulda, oughtta tell *me* these things," Manuel mimicked.

Caswell smiled, and everyone else laughed, nervously.

"We wanted to make sure we had real facts and proof. You understand," I piped up. "We'll come to you with faster updates from now on. Anything speaking to you in those photos about the guy with glasses?"

"Nothing. He's at an angle in these, and I do understand but I would appreciate faster updates. While you guys are investigating, remember I'm trying to work all of this through the law, the annoying cops who refuse to look for another suspect, and to get Jorge ready for trial." Manuel looked directly into my eyes and spoke softly.

"Well, what do we do now?" Corwin pushed up the brim of his floppy straw hat.

"Good question, Corwin. That answer will require a helluva strategy, and I think we'll need some time tonight to figure that out. Can all of you work tonight; not here but at my office? I promise to have great dinner brought in and some wine." Manuel asked.

"Sure." I spoke up first. The others agreed.

Within the hour, we all had arrived at Manuel's office. We settled into his conference room and began filling plates from a selection of whole wheat pastas, a choice of pesto or marinara sauce, meatballs for those who wanted them or eggplant parmesan. Two bottles of chianti and a dozen bottled waters were also on the table. We began to build an elaborate plan to take down Yadira, a prominent Bay Area judge, two cops, the unidentified guy and Damian Lis, and to find the real killer of Timothy Reston in the process.

"Dr. Sarah, before we start I want to ask something; should we get a police report about your window and the gunshot?" Jean asked.

Caswell answered before I could. "No, let's not do that. We don't know who on the force we can trust at this point. I'm still working on that."

"That's true," Manuel affirmed.

"I'll find out more but until then let's keep police reports and police involvement to a minimum for now," Caswell suggested.

Manuel jumped into the driver's seat of the strategy session and quickly got us organized. "With all of the excitement, I forgot what I planned to share with all of you. The autopsy came back on Timothy Reston. He died from a potassium chloride overdose. It mimics a heart attack, and because of his age and medical history, the medical examiner was suspicious. Further investigation revealed he had been injected with potassium chloride, which is a common drug in supply at prisons because it's used with another drug for lethal injections."

"Poor stupid, kid." Caswell hung his head. My mind immediately thought back to my vision of a gloved hand in a medicine cabinet. Now I knew how that vision had prepared me for this case.

"Do you think Yadira killed Timothy for some reason? Maybe she knew he was her son or he contacted her to blackmail her?" I asked. The wheels in my head were spinning.

"You know, that sounds like a possibility." Caswell seemed deep in thought, too.

"I could try to find out who adopted Timothy and what his life was like." Jean added.

"That's a good idea. And I assume you're digging deeper into Damian's life, too?" Manuel asked Jean.

"Yeah. I've had a few road blocks. His adult records are beginning to come together, but his childhood and teen years are almost non-existent. I have a lot more work to do."

"That's odd." I chimed in to assert myself. I was feeling a bit sensitive about Manuel taking over my team, because it was clear that he was taking over my team. "Jean, maybe he has an assumed name or two."

"That's a good possibility." Manuel said.

"I had asked Jean to match Damian's history to Yadira's to see where they intersect." I said.

"Good move." Manuel continued, "With that said, it is my responsibility to protect the firm. Without letting Yadira know that we're on to her, I'm going to ask our HR group to craft a carefully worded resignation to avoid conflict of interest. I'll say that I was asked by the other partners to encourage her to take a leave because of Jorge's case. She can keep her billings. Fortunately, she is not technically a partner. This will give her more time to conspire. Hopefully she'll trip up, soon."

"That's a good point," Caswell agreed. "There was some tension between them, already. We'll keep making the connection between her, Damian, the others, and Timothy. What's going to be harder is finding out who actually killed Timothy but I would put my money on Damian, right now."

"I only need reasonable doubt, but finding the killer is even better, of course." Manuel smiled.

"I can't tell. Listening to the recording; did the rest of you get the feeling the guys were setting Yadira up? They seemed to hang her out on her own with the judge. I wonder what that was about?" I offered a rhetorical question.

"Definitely sounds like a set up in the works.," Manuel agreed. "We might get lucky. That kind of disruption can give us an advantage. A weak link might want to cut a deal."

"Sounds like more surveillance?" I asked.

"Yes, but you and Corwin have to be much more careful now. Make sure you're not seen, at all," Manuel ordered. "You'll be in danger, and frankly, unless you see something crucial, don't take photos. We have enough photos."

"Yes, sir." Corwin saluted.

"I set him up with surveillance gear that gives 30 feet clear audio for recording so he can keep a safe distance and still capture what we need." Caswell explained.

Manuel slowly nodded his head. I could tell that he was impressed.

"And because my office is not safe right now, Jean, you and I will have to work from home, I guess," I suggested.

"Why not use my offices?" Manuel offered. "Sarah, you already have space here, and I'll make sure Jean has an office adjacent to yours. Our security is near impossible to get by, and we are in a high-rise, so it would be much more difficult to shoot through our windows. They can't even get into our garage, especially once I get Yadira out of the firm and have her access deactivated," he added.

"That sounds like a great idea." Jean exhaled in relief.

"That's true." I smiled.

"Something tells me that first, I need to find out whether or not Yadira knew Timothy was her biological son," Jean said.

"Exactly, Jean. And if she didn't, that information could serve as leverage to smoke out more facts in this case," Manuel instructed. "There will be a right time to make that play. It's not now, but we'll know when."

"I don't know about the rest of you, but this case has taken my appetite away. The food looks great, but I've hardly touched mine," I said.

"Not me." Caswell smacked his lips. "You guys get the best fancy-schmancy food."

"I can always have a little something. Is there champagne?" Corwin asked. We all ignored him.

"Tension makes me hungry, Sarah." Manuel laughed. "Guess I'll be eating a lot for the next few weeks. I'm disappointed in Yadira, though and I can't believe she was trying to play me. But she'll be sorry. I can guarantee that, she'll be sorry." Manuel's eyes became clear, dark steel. I knew that look. I'd seen it several times during Michael's trial. Yadira had hedged her bets, and she was about to lose.

Later that night, over the phone, Manuel and I couldn't shut off brainstorming the new developments in the case. We spent hours going over and over details. We talked about my crime kitchen recipe cards, and after laughing, he shared his spreadsheet strategic process.

"Can I ask you a nosey question?" I asked.

"Ask."

"Were you and Yadira involved? Did you date?" I dragged the words out. It was hard for me to trust any man after Michael's deception, so I had to ask.

"No, never. Yadira was like a younger sister. I took responsibility for her over the years. I don't do that often, because I have issues with trusting people. Betrayal is difficult for me. And here we go—after all these years, she's a damn criminal willing to drag my firm into her mess. Do you know how hard it is to make partner? I did. And now I'd be the one to ruin the firm's reputation in a criminal case by bringing her here. I can't believe this shit is happening."

"There's nothing I can say to make this better other than I'll help you get her," I pledged.

"You know what else is hard for me?" Manuel's tone lightened.

"No. What?" I asked.

"Watching you and wanting to just…well, I'll explain the next time I see you." Manuel laughed, a sexy laugh.

"I'll use my imagination. It's not any easier for me, you know. I see you and I want to…well, I may have to show you the next time I see you," I teased.

"Do you think it's the danger that's making us horny?" Manuel asked.

"That would be a bit sick," I giggled, "but maybe."

"Oh. Don't you have brunch with your cousin and the doctor tomorrow? Want me to come?" Manuel laughed.

"I would love for you to come, but I didn't want to ask because it'll be both boring and irritating. I thought it might jeopardize our friendship. I'll suffer through it alone, but thank you for being so generous." I chuckled.

"Ok. Well, I'll say good night for now, sexy Sarah," he whispered.

"Good night to you, hot man," I whispered back and hung up.

I went to bed happy that Manuel and I were now on the same page. It almost made the next day's Sunday brunch with Stacy and Lance bearable. Almost. But beneath all of those pleasurable thoughts, I was on edge about the elevated danger in this case. My rag-tag team had uncovered some ugly truths, the kind people would kill for in order to keep those truths buried.

CHAPTER TEN

I didn't want to deal with Ma-ma's shit, so I blew my car horn in front of her house for Stacy to come out rather than go inside and suffer through a lengthy conversation and tête-à-tête. Part of my resentment of Stacy was the way my mother protected and defended her, blindly. I also carried jealousy that dated back to our teen years. Truthfully, she was prettier, sexier, and more of a man magnet than I ever was, and I never felt good enough around her. She had made sure I kept feeling that way for our first time out together in California. Stacy had pulled out all the stops. She showed tits, ass, legs, flowing wavy hair, and hot red, thick lips. We had all the same parts; she just had more of them and advertised them better. I lowered the car window on the passenger's side and raised a fake smile.

"Hi, Stacy. Sorry for blowing, but I was running a bit late and thought we should hurry," I said.

"No problem, Sarah. Just give me time in these heels, cher." Stacy looked like an ostrich attempting to balance in her stilt-like heels, but everything moved the right way. She was wearing a skin-tight, cheetah-print dress with a swooping V-neck and flared hem with black, ankle-strapped five-inch heels. She had unusually large black hoop earrings and split her black, shoulder-length hair into a center part. Her depression and questionable suicide attempt had caused a bit of weight loss, so her waistline was smaller, accentuating her huge boobs and curvy hips. It didn't really matter what I was wearing. It was couture; expensive, but had become invisible.

"Here, I'll open the door for you." I leaned over and opened the passenger side door.

"Thank you, Sarah. Lance wanted to pick me up, but I said, no I have to ride with my couzan because she is making all of this possible for me, yeah." Stacy slowly shook her head no while talking and getting into the car.

Just then Ma-ma appeared at her window and waved bye as we drove off. I took Stacy's intentional dig in stride; she made a point to mention that Lance wanted to give her a ride. I was still in the glow of Manuel and couldn't have cared less.

"It's all good. If you want him to take you home, that's fine, too." I smiled.

I turned the volume of the radio higher to discourage conversation, but the hint was lost on Stacy.

"Sarah, you know, I'm not good alone. I have to have a man in my life. I'm not independent like you, no." Stacy talked while she rifled through her black clutch bag for a mirror and lipstick, which she added to her already painted lips.

"Stacy, it's not that I'm so independent; it's that I like being smart. I use my brains to make money. I like money. I have tons of it. So it's not that I'm focused on *not* having a man. I've dated many wonderful men and some not-so-wonderful men. It's that I like having money and choices. And I keep trying to find the love of a *good* man. So I want both, not just one of those things. I want my own money and a great man. If I already have money, I can have the man I want without feeling desperate." I was sure she had no idea what I was talking about, and then she surprised me.

"Yeah, you have the smarts to make money. I have to use my body to do that. It's just the way it is." Stacy turned to the window with a sad look. I almost felt sorry for her. Almost.

We pulled into the parking lot of Marlin's on the Bay in Berkeley and got out of the car. Waves crashing against the rocks on the marina made a romantic sound. Stacy and I walked in and I could tell that all eyes were on her. We were seated at a front-and-center table, and I motioned for Chico to come down from the stage to meet us. Chico was wearing his signature boa; this one was neon green. It adorned a bedazzled hot-pink shirt and leather pants. Chico liked to mix colors not usually worn together, but each piece of his clothing was fine fashion. He was not especially handsome, but had style. Chico was of medium brown skin and wore his hair cut short. He looked a bit like and reminded many people of the late comedian, Richard Pryor. Chico had grown up in the late '60s and '70s. He told me that he realized he was gay when he was a child. He was often bullied and beaten up so he learned to fight. Eventually, during his young adult years, he came out. Once out, he left his native Georgia and found acceptance and many lovers in the Bay Area. Our decade-old bond formed when I sang during an open mic night. Chico was the piano player with the group Relevance. He said he was mesmerized by my voice. When the group split up, he decided to remain on his own, playing piano at a number of places to make a living. These days, despite constantly claiming he needed to play piano for the money, Chico was not in any great need. He lived with a rich, white venture capitalist. They lived in the Berkeley hills in a sprawling showplace of a home.

Chico was a different kind of best friend. Our time together was spent at the club, with few visits to each other's homes. We were club siblings, not really part of the same social circles. Despite that, we loved each other dearly.

"Chico, I want you to meet my cousin, Stacy, who has recently moved here from Louisiana. Stacy, this is Chico, the amazing piano player I told you about. He is my heart friend," I said.

"Hello, Stacy." Chico offered a forced smile. He was not moved by attractive women, especially those he knew were not good to me.

"Hey, Chico. Do you always dress so gay? That's funny." Stacy put her hand to cover her mouth as she laughed.

Chico was visibly pissed. "I see that Sarah's description of you was accurate." His sneer flew directly over Stacy's head. "I have to go warm up my fingers. Sarah, let me know if you decide to come up to sing?" He smiled a nasty smile and climbed back on the stage. I was embarrassed by Stacy's ignorance. The waiter, Rob, rushed to our table.

"I'll have my usual cabernet, Rob. Stacy, what do you want to drink?"

"Jack and Coke, cher. Thank you, baby," she answered. Rob nodded, and Stacy smiled and winked at Rob, not realizing he was gay, too. His smiled inverted as he turned away from Stacy abruptly. It was interesting to watch Stacy's good looks begin to wane when partnered with her lack of social skills and unfortunate stupidity.

Lance arrived at about the same time as our drinks and picked up the tab. "Let me get these." He handed Rob cash. "Hello, beautiful ladies," he remarked as he looked at Stacy. The war had been won. Stacy had Lance's full attention. There was no way he'd ever date me again. Not that I wanted him, but Stacy didn't know that or care.

"Hey, Lance. How you doin'?" Stacy had a way of looking down in a pretend, bashful pose.

"Hi Lance," I said with pursed lips. I was over it. "You guys visit. I think I'll go join Chico on stage." I could tell where that union was headed and I didn't want to be an early witness.

"Oh, are you singing today? It will be a treat." Lance spoke to me in his signature nerd-speak sans contractions, while he leered at Stacy. I didn't bother to answer, I left the table and climbed up onstage, my wine in hand. Chico was playing "The Way You Look Tonight."

Great freakin' choice.

"That wax-faced heifer is horrible," Chico whispered. "I used to think you exaggerated about her, but she's awful. Watch her," he admonished.

"Waxed-faced?" I stifled a full gut guffaw. "The watch-her train has left the station, Chico. I've watched her my whole life, and I'm pretty sure that I don't want Lance, so she can't do any damage this time. I'm good. They appear to have a powerful attraction for each other that's kinda nauseating." I laughed.

"No shit. Beauty and the Geek. Well, let's make some music." He started playing chords.

Chico and I performed three songs. The audience went crazy with applause. I walked over to my table and interrupted Lance and Stacy deep in conversation. "Are you guys enjoying the show?" I asked.

"Oh, we're having a wonderful time. And you always had a good voice, couzan." Stacy gave a crafty smile. I could tell that she felt cocky and victorious because she now had Lance.

"Sarah, you are a wonder." Lance nodded his head in approval.

"Thank you." I smiled and thought, *Fuck you, Stacy.*

I felt my phone vibrate from inside my purse. I grabbed it.

"Hello?"

"I want to see you. Where are you?" Manuel's voice was unmistakable in its intention.

"You know, Marlin's on the Bay with Lance and my cousin, Stacy. I didn't think you'd want to—"

Manuel interrupted. "I'll be there in fifteen minutes." He hung up. I didn't inform my table mates. I just smiled and sipped my wine, swaying to the music. Manuel was about to rescue me again, this time from humiliation.

In between small talk, a few friends stopping to say hello, and being ignored by Lance and Stacy, Manuel's fifteen minutes seemed like thirty. But when he walked in, it was one of life's memorable moments. He looked like he had walked out of a magazine—tall, tan, hot, and sexy. He was wearing Armani. A black jacket that hugged his buffed body with jeans, a black shirt and black Gucci loafers. I knew Gucci when I saw Gucci. His eyes were fixed on me, and he walked straight to our table. Manuel leaned over, and his lips fit mine perfectly as he gave me a long, deep kiss. He then sat down next to me.

"Stacy, meet Manuel." I smiled. *Check-fucking-mate!*

Stacy was unable to close her mouth. Her demeanor had been cool and confident, even taunting when she appeared to be winner in the man-grab contest. But Manuel's unexpected appearance clearly knocked her off center.

"Lance, you remember Manuel, my former attorney." I reintroduced the men.

"Yes, Manuel, so great to see you again." Lance stood up and shook Manuel's hand. Lance's smile was sincere. He was unaware there was a competitive match in play. Stacy gave it a try and pushed out her bosom. "Well, Manuel, so good to meet you. I didn't realize you were coming today."

Manuel responded with a cool, impatient edge, "Thank you." And he turned his head quickly back to me. It was embarrassing. There's

85

something about the Manuels of the world; they're not enamored with the Stacy's in daylight. They want smart, attractive, classy women who can impress their bosses and peers. They would never choose a Stacy. And whether Manuel would remain in my life or not, this valuable lesson would.

The brunch righted itself into a comfortable foursome. Manuel and I, still aroused from our conversation the night before, excused ourselves early.

"Lance, Manuel and I want to call it an early Sunday; do you mind taking Stacy home?" I asked. Stacy looked as if she had eaten bad shrimp. I couldn't believe how disturbed she was because I had an attractive man interested in me and not her. She remained visibly shaken. It was pathetic, almost pathological jealousy.

"I would love to drive Stacy home, if she does not mind." Lance was still oblivious.

"Oh, that would be lovely." Stacy faked a blush.

"Great. See you guys later," I said.

"Goodbye." Manuel waved as he stood up, pulled out my chair and we left.

As we walked out, I blurted out my appreciation. "I owe you for rescuing me."

"Yes, let's see; how can you repay me? Hmm." Manuel pretended to be thinking and laughed.

"Oh, stop. That is so wrong." I hit him lightly on the arm.

"I have to say, I don't like your cousin, at all." He grinned.

"Yeah, well neither do I so you're not special." We both laughed.

He grabbed me around my waist with both hands, "Your place or mine?" He asked.

"Your place?" I asked.

"Follow me." Manuel pulled out a pen and wrote his address in the palm of my hand and then kissed it. "This is in case we get separated crossing the Bay Bridge."

I smiled. "OK."

I arrived at Manuel's San Francisco high-rise condo building and followed signs to guest parking. It was close to the lobby entrance. The concierge was good. "Ms. Jean-Louis? Mr. Cabrera has said that you are to go right up. Tenth floor, unit ten-ten." He smiled and bowed, slightly. I refused to overthink my actions. I rode the elevator, quieting my overactive mind. I didn't want to second guess this move.

The elevator door opened. I walked to the right of a wide hallway lined in impressionist art. I reached for the doorbell at unit 1010, and as I was about to ring, Manuel opened the door. He was now shirtless and wearing pants that looked a bit like surgical scrubs. His muscles flexed, his eyes razor sharp, he pulled me into his place with a steamy kiss. I dropped to my knees, untied the drawstring of his pants, and pulled them down. Without one word spoken, I embraced his manhood with my entire mouth, and it felt warm and familiar. Within minutes, Manuel reached down and scooped me up. He carried me to his enormous bed, made up with a plush gray duvet and an assortment of large, decorative pillows. The room made me think of a Mediterranean villa. Earth tones were skillfully paired with jewel tones of rich ruby red, sapphire blue, and emerald green. But the designer-obsessed amateur decorator in me fell silent as Manuel placed me softly on his bed and removed my skirt and panties. His lips met the most intimate parts of my body and caused intense heat and moisture. I coiled in weak pleasure. Somehow, this experience made sense and felt right without one word being passed between us. I let go of all inhibition and gave my entire body and soul to this man. Manuel entered me with the force of a kind animal, strong and firm. His thrusts were slow and rhythmic. It was the best sex I ever had in my life, without question. I had rapid and repeated orgasms until all of my energy was spent. I fell back into his large down pillows, exhausted. Manuel pulled out of my body and plopped down next to me, face first. We slept.

The sun bled through the tiny crevices of wood blinds. It found us on the far sides of the bed and not cuddled or with legs entwined. Manuel lifted his head and smiled. "Good morning."

"Yes, it is. A really good morning." I smiled. "I have a question."

"OK."

"Why do you think we didn't speak one word during our first time having sex? I'm just curious," I asked.

"First of all, we didn't have sex; we made love. Secondly, we don't have to talk." Manuel looked serious.

"Yes."

He got up and made strong coffee. We read the paper and spoke a little. I showered and went home. It was the most natural, exciting, and safe feeling experience I had ever had with a man. It wouldn't be the last time, not by any stretch and happened at the perfect time, right before I was to meet with my former fake fiancé at prison.

CHAPTER ELEVEN

I had never dressed to visit San Quentin before, so I had to go over the rules and guidelines that I assumed would be a bit different from my county jail visit with Jorge. Nikeba and Steve had pulled strings to help me visit Michael sooner rather than later, and the time had arrived. Two weeks from a request date was some kind of record, I was told. I decided a gray suit with a white shirt and black pumps would be boring enough. I also decided to fend off offers from nearly everyone to ride with me to San Quentin; it was important that I see Michael alone.

Getting through security clearances gave me an idea of where airline travel was headed, and after many hurry-and-waits, I was sitting with the man who had broken my heart and spirit by pretending to be my fiancé a year before. But time had placed him here without his freedom and me in a new life. Visions and a strong feeling compelled me to meet with him after he had made several requests to see me.

"You look amazing, lady." Michael's speech was slow and measured. He looked thinner and broken, but I could tell that the con artist remained in his eyes.

"Thank you. Are they making therapy available to you, as well as medication?" I asked.

"Yes, I'm on meds and weekly therapy, both individual and group," he answered.

"Is it helping?"

"Yeah, I can tell the difference. I'm more in touch with reality now. I'm still insane, but better." Michael gave a weak, goofy smile. He looked overmedicated.

"I'm not really practicing, I'm consulting on criminal cases." I said in anticipation of his curiosity.

"I know all about it. Lady, you'd be surprised at the extensive network of information that exists here on the inside. I have to tell you something." He looked over each shoulder.

"What's that?"

"You are in danger, Sarah. The word is you're a target of some high ranking drug dealers." I could barely hear Michael as he spoke softly. "Everybody in here knows about my trial and you. They tell me stuff."

"That's why you wanted to see me?" I asked.

"Yeah. I don't want to see you get killed. Ironic coming from me, but I don't. Why don't you back out of this?" He asked.

"No. This is my new work. Thanks to you and the trial, I don't have a therapy practice anymore and I see that I'm good at this. If they're talking about me, I must be better than I thought." I snapped.

"Yeah, you're stirring some shit up. I figured I wouldn't get you to back down, so I thought I might be able to help you. Listen up; the case you're on is a frame-up. The dead kid was a snitch trying to trade information for favors against some powerful people in a drug ring. A few of them heard about it and got him. They set up the other kid as some kind of revenge thing. I don't have all the details on that. But I'll send you letters." He leaned in to whisper. "I have to use some coded language because they read our mail, but I'll tell you what I hear." He flashed a toothy smile. His teeth were still perfectly straight and bright white.

"So everything about the case was intentional?" I asked.

"Yep. The whole thing was planned. The drug ring pays large, so the jailers, and some higher ups are in on it—and making some grand money. The kind of money people kill for and they're doing it. Plus, they sure as hell don't want to end up in here." Michael motioned his head around his surroundings.

"That makes sense." I nodded.

"Tell you what. Most things happening here in California, I can find out about. Let's face it, I'm a con. I'm working this place because I have to work it. I'll be here for a long time, and I should be; it's where

I belong. But while I'm here, let me send you information on your case. It's not real hard for me to keep up. Like I said, the network is extensive." Michael waited for a reaction.

"Well, I don't understand why you would want to do that."

"I don't want anything. There's nothing you can do for me. I want the work, and my mind needs the activity. I'm a dealer, and I need deals to work on, information to trade, and people to manipulate. It's what I do, Sarah. I can do this for you. And who knows, I may luck up on a deal that helps me." Michael's eyes were intense but wild-looking. He had a hustler sound to his voice. It was a bit out of character for an engineer. But he was also a narcissist and an extreme con.

And as if following a script that had been written for me, I added yet another bizarre and dangerous character to my motley crew. This one, fortunately, was already incarcerated. Somehow between all of this madness, I had hoped we could help to find the killer and free Jorge, and at the same time, justify my new strange bedfellows.

A week of work got me nowhere in the case. Mercifully, the days blew by and it was time for my brunch of choice with my girls.

"Are you fucking kidding me?" Nikeba didn't take my news well, at all. I had named and described my team of investigators at Sunday brunch with my girlfriends. Our martinis were being served, so Nikeba's sense of humor hadn't kicked in yet. But Sandy's was in annoyingly high giddy gear.

"Tell me again who is helping you investigate in a life-and-death case. Two nuts and a washed-up PI? What are you casting, a comedy?" Nikeba asked acerbically. Sandy was nearly falling out of her chair, wailing with choking laughter.

"Oh, shut up, Sandy. It's not that funny." I snapped. "I'm not casting anything. I'm maximizing my available resources." I sat up in my chair.

"The hell it isn't. I want you to take pictures of them walking down the street. Oh, that's right, one is in prison. He can't walk anywhere.

Hahaha…" Sandy started snorting laughter and had now become irritating to both of us.

"Hush, Sandy. You guys don't understand." I motioned to the waiter. "Can you bring us some bread and olive oil?" He nodded yes.

"I don't need bread and you need help," Nikeba insisted.

"Here's the deal. I can't talk specifics about the case, but research and my rare intuition aren't enough. I need people on the ground. Manuel already had the private investigator, Caswell. He gathers intelligence from law enforcement. Corwin…"

"Corwin? A-hahahahaha!" Diners at nearby tables turned around when Sandy shouted Corwin's name and spit her martini with laugher.

"Yes, Corwin. We all know that he follows people. So he's doing surveillance." I tried to lend an air of dignity to my decision.

"That would be called a transfer of his stalking skills?" Nikeba was amused and now giggling, herself.

"Somewhat. Now, Jean is research and Michael is doing intelligence work from inside the system, let's say."

"He's a snitch." Nikeba shook her head.

At that point, I started giggling at my own explanations. "I have to admit, it's bizarre, but believe it or not, they're all gathering impressive information. Oh, what the hell. I give up. I can't make this sound normal." I gave in and joined their rolling laughter.

"Well, that's the best laugh I've had in weeks. But let's get to the important stuff. Have you done Manuel yet?" Sandy asked.

"Wow. Subtle. And yes. We have crossed the line from platonic friendship to friends with benefits. Sure was nice." I smiled and fought a look of guilt.

"Sarah, I love Manuel. He is a dear friend; just know that he has not been one to make a commitment in relationships. He's a great guy, but that's been his track record," Nikeba warned, gently.

"I know, and for now, I can't say that matters. I'm fine working the case and getting to know him. After my wedding plans crashed last year, I can wait on trying the commitment part again myself." I shrugged.

"We understand." Nikeba and Sandy looked down.

"And as if life isn't unpredictable enough, I told you my cousin Stacy lives here now. Well, she's dating—get this—Lance," I announced. "She wanted you guys to come to a jazz brunch last week, but I spared you by making up excuses. It was the Stacy and Lance show," I explained.

"I thought Lance was smarter than that," Sandy shot out.

"Wow, that sounds mean, like something I would've said." Nikeba chuckled.

"It does, doesn't it?" Sandy marveled.

"I have a theory," I started. "I think that although Lance is a handsome man now, he was probably that thick glasses wearing nerd whom nobody wanted to date. So even though he's a doctor now, nerd-boy in his subconscious remembers when girls that look like Stacy ignored him all through his teen and college years. A trophy like Stacy means he has arrived." I raised my glass.

"Bullshit. He has a weak ego, and he's horny. She's probably a quick fuck," Nikeba blurted.

We all blurted out loud laughter.

"Sarah, even though Lance stepped up when you needed him for trial, I've never thought much of him. He reminds me of those overly-nice, chicken shit guys with no balls. The way he acted after you guys accidentally slept together was gutless and charmless. I'm glad you're not with him." Nikeba vented.

"Yeah. I hate to agree with Nikeba, but Lance was cruel to you." Sandy said.

"He was a jerk, but fast forward to today and who cares?" I added.

"I know I don't," Nikeba volunteered.

"Not a bit," said Sandy.

We got caught up on each other's lives and filled up on coffee before leaving for our homes. "Monday morning will get here too fast for me. Bye, girls!" We all waved and drove off.

I walked into my place and to a living room floor now filled with crime kitchen recipe cards. I reread each card, refreshing my memory of the players in this case, their backgrounds, and their roles, as far as we knew. Once I had settled into my slippers and the softness of home, I decided to call upon my visions for wisdom and protection.

"I am protected from the evil you send my way. You have no power over me today or any day." I repeated the chant three times while I held a tiny doll image of Yadira. I had created a gris-gris doll for protection from her. I didn't push a pin into it because I couldn't bear to wish her harm, I only asked that any power she had would wither away. I wanted to make sure she couldn't harm me. I lit candles and incense, turned on my Gregorian chants, and commanded, "Tell me what I need to know, and show me all that I need to see; there is truth deep within, and it's trying to hide itself from me." I repeated that phrase three times and sat with eyes closed. Within minutes the taste of dead animals crept from the back of my tongue to the front of my mouth. Sour, bitter saliva became thick in my mouth, and my head swirled with dizzying pain. My stomach turned and churned, and I feared I would pass out. Vivid images began to play in my mind's eye. I saw myself going toward young Timothy again in the foot steps of the killer. This time I saw the whole room. I saw Jorge asleep in the upper bunk. I saw my gloved hands holding a syringe. The gloves were black leather, like motorcycle or driving gloves. The syringe was primed, and as I lunged it into a vein in Timothy's neck, his eyes bulged in surprise and disbelief. Before he could yell for help, my left hand covered his mouth tightly while my right hand emptied the contents of the syringe into his struggling body. Within minutes, he had given up and went limp, eyes still wide open. I walked out of the cell; a jailer smiled and gestured OK. I walked out of the building, got onto a motorcycle, and left. The vision faded. I pulled new recipe cards and wrote every piece of the vision I could remember. I called Manuel.

"Hello?"

"Manuel, I just had a long, full vision that tells more of the story. Is this a good time for you to hear it?" I asked.

"Of course; let me get something to take this down, hold on."

While Manuel searched, I had the feeling someone was outside of my door. When he returned to the phone, I spoke softly, "Manuel.

Someone is outside my door. I can tell. I hear them." My voice and body were shaking.

"I'm on my way," he said.

"No, I'll call security. I should go to the peep hole and..."

"*No.* Do not stand in front of that door. I'm calling your building security with my other phone, right now, and I'm on my way. Stay on the line with me. Go into your bedroom or bathroom and lock the door. Do you have a gun?" Manuel had strict focus.

"No, I don't have a gun. Oh, wait. I hear voices now. Oh my God, what's happening? Manuel, I'm scared," I whispered.

"I know, baby. But stay on the phone with me. I'm in my car now and nearing the bridge. Your security may be one of the voices. I called them. Just stay with me," Manuel insisted.

I had gone into my bathroom, but the loud arguing got the better of my curiosity. I went back into my living room. I jumped when a loud sharp sound hit the door. "Oh shit, Manuel! Something hit the door." Tears were now streaming down my face as I trembled.

"I'm not that far away, baby. Try to stay calm and away from the door. Your security has probably confronted them," he said.

Clack! Clack!

There were more sharp bumps against my front door. But this time, one voice had a familiar sound. I listened closer and heard the unmistakable voice of Corwin, protesting a demand that he leave the building. I walked closer to the door and was able to clearly hear his highbrowed indignation.

"I am a friend and colleague of Dr. Jean-Louis, you peasant! I'm working on a case. Dr. Sarah! Dr. Sarah! Please tell this rent-a-cop that you know me!" Corwin yelled.

"Sir, sir. Calm down," the security guard said.

I spoke into my cell phone to a listening Manuel. "Manuel, it's Corwin. He's arguing with building security," I said.

"Corwin? What the hell is he doing in your hallway?" Manuel asked. "I'm parking now; don't open your door until I get up there." He hung up.

Security rang. "Ms. Jean-Louis, we apologize for the noise and chaos in your hallway. We found a potential intruder at your door and he insists he knows you. A Mr. Corwin? And Mr. Cabrera is here as well, asking to come up."

"Yes, they are both fine." The tense moments had finally melted into relief and untied the knots in my stomach. When I heard Manuel at the door, I opened it and let him and Corwin inside.

The guard apologized. "Sorry for the noise, Ms. Jean-Louis." He went back downstairs.

"What the fuck were you doing?" Manuel's eyes darted in Corwin's direction, his fists clenched. Corwin sat down at my table, crossed his panty-hose-covered legs, swallowed hard, and began his explanation. "I was watching Dr. Sarah's place. After our meeting I thought I better watch over her place; you know, the way someone shot at the office and shot at you, and this case is becoming so dangerous," Corwin's voice reached into an upper range. "Well, when I was outside, I saw a guy on a motorcycle, and he sneaked into the building. He had pried open a side door of this building. I saw him. I was suspicious of him, so I went into the lobby and told the guard. But rather than listen to me, they kept telling me to get out of the building." Corwin took in a deep breath.

I was pretty sure Corwin's protective hat for the evening didn't help his credibility. He was wearing a white pillbox hat like those made famous by former first lady, Jackie Kennedy in the 1960s.

"Well, when I saw my chance, I sneaked into the elevator and came up here; and when I got off of the elevator, who was at Dr. Sarah's door, but the motorcycle guy? I shouted at him to stop. He pushed me against her door and then ran away down the stairwell. The elevator opened, and security came up and pushed me against the door a few times, roughing me up while they asked what I was doing up here. That's what happened. I swear." There was both innocence and insanity in Corwin's voice.

"Manuel, you can believe Corwin. Mr. Corwin, I appreciate you looking out for me, but let me know next time. Why don't you go home and rest? You've done enough work for tonight," I said.

"Thank you. Dr. Sarah. I am overwhelmed. I think I need a cup of tea. Good night." Corwin looked Manuel up and down, re-positioned his pillbox hat, and walked out with the straightened posture of an aristocrat.

"Are you sure you can trust him?" Manuel looked perplexed.

"No, of course I'm not sure, but I needed him to leave because I have to tell you about my vision and how the motorcycle rider he talked about was part of it. Let's sit down. Wine?" I pulled a cab from my wine rack and motioned for Manuel to join me at the dining table while I opened it and poured.

"The motorcycle thing makes sense?" he asked.

"Yes. Here's what I was trying to tell you over the phone." I gave Manuel the details of my vision.

"So as you were in the shoes and perspective of the killer, you evidently had the assistance of one of the jailers and then left on a motorcycle. It fits with what we got in the ME's report. Timothy had enough potassium chloride in his system to kill a large elephant. He went into a coma before he died." Manuel was deep in thought. "No syringe was left behind and no fingerprints."

"We're starting to close in on what really happened. The good news is, I can call for a vision or for insight, but the bad news is, if it continues to put me in the shoes of the perpetrator, it is a helluva lot harder to solve the crime, because I can't see the face of whose committing it." I shook my head.

"But don't sell yourself short. We know now that we have two people to smoke out: a motorcycle rider who's our killer and a jailer who's an accessory. That's more than we had yesterday. And in his own way, crazy Corwin helped to get us there, I have to admit." Manuel smiled for the first time since he had arrived. We finished off the bottle of cabernet.

"Let's put this case on hold for now." Manuel smiled again.

I didn't need a vision to know what the second smile meant. I put away our glasses and led the way to my bedroom.

CHAPTER TWELVE

I woke up to the smell of Manuel, a soft mix of day-old Acqua di Parma Colonia Ambra and sweat. Manuel's fragrance preferences were as meticulous as his fashion. His fragrance wardrobe consisted of Dunhill Icon during the week because of his love of their bottle. On weekends, I could smell Hermès Equipage Géranium by day, and by night, Acqua di Parma Colonia Ambra. Although I preferred one Chanel fragrance as my signature, Manuel and I were otherwise fashion compatible and couture conscious. I loved that his closet was as overrun as mine. I sucked in my stomach and tried to slide from under his muscle-toned right arm to make coffee, but I woke him.

"Good morning, corazon." Manuel whispered into my ear, kissed me, and went for the shower. "You did notice that I brought clothes last night, right?" He yelled from the bathroom while turning the water on full blast.

"Yes, I did. Your bag is still in the living room," I yelled back.

"Right. Grab it for me," he ordered. Well, it was official. I was no longer the new girl you impress. I was now the established girl who fetches. I smiled to myself. The Monday rush was a mélange of phone calls in between getting dressed, a scant breakfast of coffee and sprouted-grain toasted bread with jam, and the sprint to our cars in my parking garage.

"See you at the office." Manuel kissed me lightly on the lips and slammed the door of his silver 911 Porsche. He zoomed off before I even started my car.

After that bullet had been fired into my office, Jean and I worked out of Manuel's law office. The gunshot had loosened my otherwise stubborn tendency to prefer my own digs. I walked in to the background sounds of a law office. "Good morning, this is Slovenksy, Hickelstein, Mason, and Cabrera; may I help you?" was coming from several reception bays. I smiled at the attendants and made way to my office as I passed and nodded at Jean who looked settled in hers.

"Good morning, Dr. Sarah. IT stopped by and helped to get me back on the network. We were having a few problems earlier, but…" Jean's efficiency comforted me, but I stopped listening to her because I knew all would be well. No matter how dangerous or drastic change would come about, she remained steady. I had to wonder why in the world she continued to work for me with my bizarre life, but then again, I paid her a lot of money. I chuckled to myself. Before I dove deeper into sentiment, loud voices interrupted my thoughts. Jean and I looked in the direction of an argument and the sound of something slammed onto a desk. It came from Manuel's office.

"Think what you would do if you were one of the partners here, Yadira. This case and your involvement are a bit cozy. You only have a short tenure here; you're too involved, and this, frankly, is a negative on the firm's reputation." Manuel's voice was cold and not as familiar as it had been with Yadira.

"How dare you and those snobs look down on me because of Jorge? And you of all people, Manuel!" Yadira shouted.

"Me of all people what, Yadira? What? Because you've done so much for me? Name it. What exactly have you done for me? When?"

"Oh, you don't want me to talk about what I've done for you, Manuel. Not here, not now." Yadira threatened.

"Don't give me that crap! But I can begin the list of how I've helped, truly helped and supported you, even by bringing you here. Yes, this is bad stuff, and we have a firm's reputation to protect. It's bigger than you—or me, for that matter." Manuel's voice carried an edge of anger.

"Well, I'm glad to find out how you really feel and what a snob you have become. I will remove my burden from your life." Yadira stomped off to her office, threw folders inside the door, and shouted back to Manuel, "And you can send my things to my home. Screw you and the partners!" Yadira grabbed her purse and stormed out, slamming the glass door to the offices. They vibrated.

There's a quiet facade of normalcy after a dramatic office scene that is usually overplayed. That held true as coworkers conducted drawn-out conversations about the copy machine and were overly helpful with coffee and other nonessential tasks to mask the discomfort of the awkward confrontation. Jean and I said nothing but looked at each other knowingly. We went back into our respective offices. As soon as I sat down, Manuel's assistant, Janelle, buzzed to tell me he wanted to see me.

"Have a seat, and please close the door," Manuel instructed. I sat, feeling a bit of the school principal's office, although I didn't think I had done anything wrong.

"Did I do something?" I asked.

Manuel slowly revealed a big smile. "Of course not. I had conversations early this morning with the partners, following the e-mail alerts I had sent about this situation. They wanted her out without even knowing all of the details. What I shared was enough for them. They're fine with them as clients, but not her inside of the firm. She could probably fight us, but with the level of guilt she's carrying for other crimes, she's better off leaving without any thought of taking legal action against this firm or me." Manuel sat back in his chair.

"She obviously doesn't give a damn about this firm. That was clear from the recordings. She was only here to sabotage the case where she could, so I guess that's what really pissed her off," I said.

"Definitely. She wanted to be on the inside of this case to keep tabs on what we would learn. I have to get her credentials and firm access immediately cut off. I'm glad to have this part over and done. Thanks to your team." Manuel looked at me with soft eyes.

"I hate to say it, but I had a bad feeling about her the day I met her." I stared at Manuel, hungry to see a reaction to my remark about Yadira. But I got nothing as he held a poker face. I wondered what she meant about him not wanting people to know how she helped him. I would wait for another time to ask about that.

"Well, now we can move on to finding the real killers. I'm going to meet with Jorge at the jail this afternoon. We've gone over his story a million times, but I've got to keep his spirits up and make sure the cops don't trip him up. Are you planning to pull your crew together? I really need to get somewhere more substantial in this case." Manuel looked frustrated.

"Yes—in fact, I want them to come here for a meeting this week. We're thinking that we need to come up with a way to go ahead and set that group of suspects up."

"I've been thinking the same thing. We're not quite there yet, but we're going to need to do something like that fairly soon," Manuel agreed.

I stood up. "OK. Let me check with Caswell and see what's new with them. I'll get you an update."

"And Sarah, please be careful," Manuel warned. "We thwarted their plan and seem to be getting closer to something so this will likely become more dangerous. Don't go anywhere alone, and don't take chances. Maybe we need to get security for you since the motorcycle rider broke into your building."

"No, I promise I'll be careful." I walked out of his office, deceptively steady.

The Stacys of the world can't take a victory without an audience. While Manuel, my crew, and I worked on a life and death case, Stacy was working on Lance to secure her future. They had become inseparable and she seemed to want everyone to know it was going her way. After only a few weeks of dating, I received an invitation from them to a jazz brunch at a restaurant in Berkeley. I had spent the past weeks literally under Manuel and couldn't give a shit. Stacy called to make sure I would attend and invite a few friends.

"Oh, Ti-Sarah, I sure hope you can come. I found the cutest little place on San Pablo in Berkeley one weekend when Lance and me was shopping. We stopped there for lunch, and I said, 'Lance, this is the kind of place we need to do a Sunday brunch, and look they have a jazz group that plays on Sundays.' And Lance was excited, too. So we said, we could invite people here and when could we do this, and so..." Stacy was one long, run-on sentence on the other end of the phone while I timed my "ah-has" and "oh yeahs" perfectly. I took note of her new found obsession with Sunday jazz brunches, though. I saw it as an attempt to imitate my life. Without fully realizing it, I had committed to going and said I'd ask Manuel to attend. In the midst of an intense case, this bullshit seemed a worthless distraction.

"OK, Stacy. Well, I'm at work, so I better go." I begged off of the phone.

"Oh yeah, cher. I understand. I'll see you soon. Have a good day. Bye-bye."

Great, now I have to spend more time with the nutty professor and the nut. I shook off the conversation and refocused on my work.

The week of no news and no results had dragged on. My team seemed cursed with rabbit holes and empty trails. It was as if someone was placing fake, complicated leads in our paths to mock us with busy work. We hadn't turned up the new, hot facts we needed, so I hated to ask a frustrated Manuel to a party with Stacy and Lance. But I went for it anyway one day at the office.

"I know we have so much work to do, but if we can just make an appearance, it would be a huge favor to me," I whined a little.

"It's OK. I like it when you owe me." He sported a quick, devious smile.

"I've noticed that I keep ending up in the debt column with you; don't I?" We joked a few more minutes in the hallway and then went to our respective offices. I sensed that everyone at the firm knew we were involved, but we tried to keep it professional in front of them.

Once at my desk, I pored over and over photos, notes, and records, determined to find something that I had possibly overlooked. I stopped on one of Corwin's photos of Yadira, Damian, the judge, and the others in their covert meetings. This time something got my attention. I honed in on Damian's jawline, and I struggled to remember where I had seen it before. Jean walked in and broke my train of thought.

"I have a message for you. It was left at the reception desk out front. No phone number was left with it. It just has your name on it." Jean looked uneasy.

I looked up. "What is it?"

She passed me the index card sized note, which was written in all capital letters. It read:

IF YOU WANT INFORMATION, MEET ME OUTSIDE WHERE THE OLD KDIA RADIO STATION BUILDING USED TO BE AT THE BAY BRIDGE TOLL PLAZA, 10 O'CLOCK TOMORROW NIGHT. COME BY YOURSELF OR I WON'T TELL YOU A THING. I'M IN TOO DEEP AND NEED A WAY OUT.
—You'll know who when you see me!

The "you'll know who" was the only signature.

Before Jean could ask, I answered, "I'm going."

"Well then, dammit, I'm calling an emergency meeting of the guys. We need to let them know this." Jean stormed out and returned to her office. I knew she was mad at me for taking this kind of risk.

My phone rang shortly after she left. "Dr. Sarah, Corwin and Caswell want you to meet them at The Diner between one o'clock and one thirty." Jean hung up abruptly.

"Well, thank you," I talked to the dead phone.

"You can't! I won't let you. I didn't protect you last time but I will protect you this time." Corwin pounded his finger into the table for emphasis.

"Keep your voice down, Mr. Corwin, and don't you think you're exaggerating a bit?" I asked.

"OK, so maybe he's a little dramatic but Doc Sarah, he makes a point. This is a dangerous case with high stakes, a judge and all. And we can tell from the tapes they got a taste for murder." Caswell weighed in, his New Jersey accent heavier for some reason.

"On the other hand, this case is as stale as day old bread. We keep following these people and we got pictures but nothing to connect them to the murder yet. Sometimes I wonder if they know we's following them. We're gettin' nowhere. Maybe we need to poke the bear a bit; you know?" Caswell made a poking motion with his hand and looked at us for agreement.

Jean was visibly upset. "I just hate it when Dr. Sarah is the bait. Why her? We don't even know who the note is from." Jean folded her arms and sat back in the booth.

"Ok. Here's what we'll do. We'll put a wire on Doc Sarah," Caswell began.

"Boy, that sounds familiar." I rolled my eyes up to the ceiling.

Caswell looked confused, but continued. "We put a wire on you and I'll be near the toll plaza, hiding behind the building. We can't let you go by yourself. That's out of the question," he insisted.

I looked up and thought for a minute. "OK. But nobody tell Manuel. He can't know about this yet, because he wouldn't want me to go and he'd interfere. We need to see what we can find out from this."

The twenty-four hours that followed were torturous. By nine o'clock Tuesday night, I was at home being wired by one of Caswell's PI friends, a woman.

"Now, be careful not to move this wire, it's the tricky one. But everything else is tight." She smoothed her hands over the tape on my back.

"Now, let's check the sound." The sound check took me back to a year earlier and the dangerous confrontation in Michael's case. My mind drifted as she conducted the tests. She packed up her things and wished me well. It was time for me to go to the darkest, creepiest area of the Bay Bridge. I got into my car and wondered if it was time to consider buying a gun if I survived this ordeal. Manuel's name appeared on the screen of my mobile phone, but I didn't dare answer. I didn't want him to know about this rendezvous.

While my right foot kept steady on the accelerator, my left leg shook nervously. It took a short fifteen minutes for me to see the frontage road along the bridge, and while I expected an abandoned shack off the road to be draped in darkness it showed the reflection of headlights. *That must be my anonymous connection.* I exited and drove slowly along the road toward the lights. As I got closer, my heart jumped into my throat. I saw the silhouette of a motorcycle and a helmeted rider with black gloves! *Oh shit, I'm being set up to be killed!*

I slammed my breaks and put my car in reverse. I didn't have a full exit plan, but I was haphazardly attempting to get back up onto the freakin' freeway. While I looked back and forward to achieve this reverse maneuver, a military looking green hummer flew past me off road. Within seconds it slammed into the motorcycle, ejecting the driver into the air like a puppet and onto the ground. It backed up to roll over the driver again and continued forward onto the freeway. *Oh my God! I just watched a murder! Oh my God. Oh my God!*

Fear and survival took me over. I lunged my car forward and settled for the first exit at Treasure Island for a turnaround back to Oakland. I ordered my mobile phone to call Jean. My voice was layered with weeping and talking at the same time. "Jean, Jean. It's awful, Jean."

"Dr. Sarah! What? Where are you? I'll call the police." Jean was shouting.

I continued to weep. "It's not me. It's not me. I'm in my car and alone. Someone hit the person who was waiting for me. The person they hit was on a motorcycle."

"Who was it, Dr. Sarah?"

"I don't know. It was so fast. It was so fast." I moaned while wiping tears and trying to drive without hitting anyone. "I'm about to pass by there again."

"Why the hell are you going back?" Jean rarely cursed.

"I'm not going back. I had to go forward and take a turnaround at Treasure Island. Oh, shit! There are a ton of police cars. I bet Caswell is over there somewhere."

"I'm relieved it's not you, Dr. Sarah. Could you tell anything about the motorcycle driver." Jean asked. She was now crying.

"No, but wait. I've slowed down with the other looky loos. I see the body of the driver being lifted on the stretcher and a pony tail is hanging off. Holy shit, Jean. I think that's Yadira." Tears overtook my ability to speak.

"Don't try to talk anymore. Focus on driving. I'm headed to your place and I'll meet you in the lobby. Come straight home. I'm calling the others. This is too much." Jean sniffled and hung up.

I grabbed my steering wheel tightly leaving the colorful flashing lights of highway patrol in my rearview mirror. Both of my legs shook with fear and guilt. I wondered if my gris-gris doll of Yadira had led to this. And I wondered if the treatment from Ms. Lorena was a dangerous tool that was now part of me. I decided I would tell no one about that doll, not even Ma-ma. I gratefully exited to West Grand Avenue and made it home.

About an inch of Corwin's striped pajama pant showed under the right leg of his khakis. "Jean scared the hell out of me. She said it was an emergency involving you and to get over here right away. What's happened?" Corwin was shaken and wiped his eyes with a handkerchief.

Even Caswell was ruffled. "I got to the toll plaza a little late and saw your car trying to back up and then shoot forward. A little after that I saw highway patrol and all hell broke loose. I saw you double back so I followed your car." He was breathing heavy. Jean had arrived with her hair in perfectly parted sections of hairpin-covered circular curls, the way hair was set in the 1960s. "I had to get you guys here as fast as possible so you could hear Sarah tell you what happened."

I described the scene to the group while I fixed myself a vodka rocks. "Serve yourselves." I downed half my drink. "That hummer came from behind me and careened into the motorcycle. The poor woman was thrown about six feet into the air. Then run over again. Dear God. It was awful to see." I shook my head.

"Holy shit! They got her." Caswell made his signature circular motion with his right hand and then ended it with pulling an imaginary trigger. "But who, why, and what was her part in this?"

Jean had taken it upon herself to call Manuel. He got the same emergency message. Security let him up. He was on my list of approved visitors.

"What happened?" Manuel bolted in with a look of panic I hadn't seen from him before. Jean started answering by telling him about the note. Caswell told him about the wire and how he went along, and then I told how I saw Yadira die. "Then we all met up here." I looked at Manuel and sniffled.

He paused. "I could kill you myself!" Manuel was more pissed than the first day I met him.

"I know. I should have told you about this…" I started to speak to a pacing Manuel.

"Shut up! Are you fucking crazy? Are you crazy, Sarah?" Manuel glared. The others followed Manuel's pacing with their eyes and followed our conversation with the panning heads of a tennis match.

"But this is why I didn't…" I tried a second time to complete a sentence.

"Do not talk. Don't talk. Did you not learn a thing last year?" Manuel pointed his index finger straight into the air. "You could've been killed. You could've been set up to be implicated in a crime. You don't know what you could've walked into. I…" Manuel put his index finger to his lips, turned his head to one side, and fell back onto my sofa, blowing out air in speechless frustration.

I waited a few seconds and then tried again. "You would not have agreed, and I wouldn't have been able to dig deeper."

"Deeper? Do you have any idea how dangerous this goddamn case is? These people are playing for keeps. Hell, they've killed Yadira, and she was one of them. Why do you take ridiculous and unnecessary risks with your life? Do you think you have more than one life? Is that what you think? What? Tell me! I'm at a loss as to why anyone with full brain capacity would do some shit like this." Manuel was fuming. His eyes were large, dark and round with anger. I kept quiet and looked down.

"Manuel. Maybe you can give her a break. She was just trying to help," Caswell was sympathetic.

"I know you're trying to help, Caswell, but don't. Sarah should know better." Manuel wouldn't budge. "Give us a minute, guys. Sarah, your room." Manuel motioned to the hallway. I walked to my room as Manuel followed. Once in the bedroom, I turned around to face him, nervously.

"You won't let me talk, so you talk," I pouted.

"Sarah, you promised that you'd be especially careful during this case and not take chances. I don't appreciate you telling me one thing and then doing another. I care about you and it's upsetting that you'd take this kind of risk. It makes me wonder about your judgment." Manuel shook his head.

"So, you think I'm stupid now?" I made a shift from nervous to pissed off.

"I think that decision was not very bright." Manuel held his jaw firmly.

I spoke in my slowly enunciated, Oakland-style-hella-angry cadence. I punched out key words for emphasis. "Well, when a case has gone stale, it can take unconventional methods to get new information. Or, you can sit on your safe ass and get nowhere while a young man's life is in your hands." I raised my voice and readied for a good fight.

"I know damn well what's at stake for my client. In fact, I helped a client last year despite the silly shit she kept doing. Are you trying to insult me as a lawyer? Because you're in no position to judge me, either." Manuel's voice elevated, he had his hands on his hips.

"Well, don't try to judge me, you arrogant wind bag! I don't need some man to tell me what to do!" I let go.

"Don't call me names. You overgrown child! And evidently, somebody needs to tell you what common sense looks like." Manuel shouted, full power.

"Well, fuck you!" I yelled.

"Fuck you!" He yelled back.

"Fuck you!" I kept pace.

"Well, fuck you!" he shouted.

"After this case, I don't ever want to see your mean, chauvinist oinking ass again!" I shrieked.

"Works for me. And you can park your broom at your own office!" He made a pointing motion as if toward my office.

"Bite me," I retorted, shoved past him, and walked back into the living room.

"Shrew," Manuel said under his breath as he followed.

"Beast," I said under my breath.

As Manuel and I walked back into the living room, it was obvious the others had heard every word of our fight. They were visibly uncomfortable. Jean pretended to scan through a two-month-old magazine. I straightened my shirt. Manuel ran his hand through his hair. We both tried to act as if our loud argument had happened in secret.

I cleared my throat and steadied my voice. "Well, do you guys remember a while back we thought that Damian and the other guys were setting Yadira up? It looks as if we were on to something with that; huh?" I got the meeting started.

"You know, that's true. They were hanging her out to dry, for sure," Caswell added. "Looks like what we heard in the recording was a big part of the setup. We could assume that she sent the note for your meeting, Doc Sarah. But, it's also possible somebody else sent it to make sure you would see what happened to Yadira. A kind of intimidation."

"You're right, Caswell. And we just don't know." Manuel seemed dazed as he spoke.

I was ready to push further. "Our next move may be the most difficult we've had so far. But, I think we have to set one of them up to make some progress in smoking out the real killer and getting Jorge off," I went on.

"Yeah. We need them to start turning on each other," Manuel agreed.

"That's a tried-and-true police tactic. And then somebody might be inspired to cut a deal." Caswell nodded in support.

"Well, I think it's time for me to follow that Damian now." Corwin was determined.

"Nooo." The room hummed with a group bellow.

"The man is dangerous. He may have killed Yadira and Timothy. We have to think this through," I insisted.

Manuel stepped up and took charge of the room, and despite our post argument anger I felt good about it. "Let's take some time and organize the logical next steps." He said.

While I had had the bright idea to trip up our fiends with some form of disruption, I didn't have any real contributions on how to get that accomplished. I looked to the ceiling for invisible inspiration. I wasn't alone. Caswell also looked to the imaginary heavens, blowing air out of his mouth in frustration. Jean stared at her notepad, doodling in nearly perfect circles. And Corwin was comparing his two hands like a five year old.

Manuel broke the brief silence. "OK. Sarah, maybe you can try to get in contact with Michael. See if you can get a call in to him with Nikeba's help. See if he has any inside information on Yadira's death. Corwin, you follow the judge and see if there's anything that turns up there. Check out who he meets with and anything else. Caswell, work more sources on Damian Lis. And Jean, time to step up a records search on Lis. Try everything you can. I'm going to work inner channels on the judge. I want his ass." Manuel had cold anger in his shining, dark eyes. We all said good night. I wished they could've stayed over at my place. The case had become a nightmare and I felt more like a target. My fight with Manuel meant there was no chance he would spend the night with me so I locked up, cleaned up, and went to bed, wide awake.

It only took Nikeba and Steve a few days after the confirmation of Yadira's death to get me a phone call arranged with Michael. I was in my office at Manuel's firm when I accepted his collect call.

"I wish you would bring me some cigarettes," Michael said.

As he didn't smoke, I realized it had to be his coded language. I kept listening. "Ah, I know what you're thinking, but stop. They're not as dangerous as people say. That's bullshit. They're second hand dangerous, though." Then Michael broke into forced laughter. "I think that fucking tequila I used to drink was a silent killer, but I stopped it. I was fucking myself up all these years. So tequila had to go, had to go. But I can't have that anyway. Just bring me some cigarettes, and I'm cool." Michael seemed done.

"I'll try to get back there soon," I said.

"Yeah, you do that, but you'll catch the devil first. Go ahead. Catch you later." He hung up. Having learned my lesson about keeping any information about the case from Manuel, I called his assistant and asked if I could see him. I told Janelle it was urgent.

"He can see you now." Janelle called me back within minutes. I walked down the hall to Manuel's office.

"Dr. Jean-Louis." Manuel was cold and professional.

"Mr. Cabrera." I returned the frost. "I spoke with Michael and have written down the code." Manuel sat up and dropped his guard a little. He showed immediate interest as I pushed my notepad toward him.

"OK. Great. Let's see what we have." He tried to read my notes. Manuel stared at the words, repeating them. We continued to repeat possible formulas, none of which seemed to make any sense.

Finally, Manuel stood up. "I got it!" he declared. "Cigarettes. Philip Morris. That's code for Judge Philip Ackers. Cigarettes represent the judge. Tequila is obviously Yadira. The devil has to be for Damian. Damian Lis. So let's see. Ackers is not as dangerous as he seems. Yadira is a silent killer, whatever that entails. And he's telling us that we have to catch Damian. Wow." Manuel was deep in thought.

"That makes sense. Yadira was a motorcycle rider, but so is the man who broke into my building. Did Yadira kill Timothy or set up these crimes or did someone else? Is Damian a killer or maybe if caught, he would give up everyone else? Whew. This isn't as obvious as I thought it would be," I said.

"Remember, in order to help, Michael has to be careful and cunning. He likely has buried information within this dialogue. We have to keep examining it." Manuel looked away.

"Are you OK?" I leaned in a bit. "This is such a huge disappointment for you. You thought she was a friend," I said.

"Shit happens. Yadira was a shitty woman." And with that, Manuel shut down and got back to work. I took the hint and left his office. But I wasn't satisfied with that. I turned around and found the courage to walk back into his office. He looked up, still a bit chilly.

"Can I help you with something?"

"Yes. I had the beginnings of a relationship of sorts with this hot, brilliant lawyer. It all went to hell over a work-related argument, and he wants me to move out of his office. I don't want to do that. I don't know what to do. Any advice?" It was a brave move for me, given my history of avoidance.

Manuel's eyes softened. His tight jaw loosened, and a tiny curl of a smile framed the ends of his mouth. "Well, I think if you apologize, nicely…"

"Apologize?" I cut in, and my back straightened.

Manuel stood up and walked toward me. He made a shush signal with his finger. "Apologize and promise to never do it again, but instead do a few other things and the hot lawyer might apologize, too. That might help you two to work something out. Just sayin'—you know." Manuel smiled like a mischievous teenager.

"Oh, well. I'm so very sorry that I yelled at you and called you names." I whispered. Manuel was standing in front of me, holding my neck with both hands, kissing me repeatedly.

"And I will do other things, but I need to know what they are."

"I apologize for calling you names, dear Sarah. And I accept your apology." A long kiss interrupted his narrative. "And this office is not the place to give you your task list. But you will get one from me, and we'll use that list to get back on track." He smiled.

"I'm sure I'll be working for this," I said softly, smiling.

"Like you've never worked before." Manuel laughed. We both laughed.

"I better go." I kissed Manuel and broke free.

"Yeah, you better." He chuckled.

"Oh, can you do a conference call with me and the team so we can bring them up to speed on Michael's coded message?"

"Sure. Give me about ten minutes or so," he replied. "I have some police officers coming in to get information from us about Yadira and cases she was working on. They were tipped off she was targeted for a hit."

"Wow. I wonder who tipped them off." I laughed.

"Oh, probably someone with a few employees with different voices who called from another number besides his office." Manuel gave me a sly smile. "The dirty cops may still get a chance to swing the ruling of her death to an accident, but I had to try."

"I don't blame you."

Back in my office, I took a few minutes to quietly cheer our reconciliation. I had hoped it would stick. My track record with men wasn't impressive. I returned my mind to work mode and asked Jean to set up the conference call. I shared Michael's code language with Jean,

Caswell, and Corwin when the call began. Manuel had joined the call by phone from his office. We all decided to continue to try and solve Michael's puzzle. Manuel told the group how he had just met with police and tried to steer them to suspicion about Yadira's death. Caswell said he heard from his contacts some cops were already calling Yadira's murder an unfortunate motorcycle accident.

"An accident? That's bullshit. I saw it." I challenged.

"We know but the last thing you need to be is a witness," Caswell said.

"Exactly. Stay under the radar." Manuel was firm.

"Well, I picked up something," Corwin reported. "I've been following the judge, and I heard him talking on his cell phone, walking to the courthouse. I overheard him make dinner plans with Damian Lis. I'm planning to go the restaurant and try to record their conversation. I can probably get a table near them. They're going to Canary's, and I have a long history with the maître d' there. I'll push him a few bucks to give me a good table. Do you want to go, Dr. Sarah?" Corwin asked.

Manuel answered for me. It kind of pissed me off. "Absolutely not. Sarah is now a full-fledged target. You bring us the audio and we won't need much more after this." Manuel ordered.

"Please be careful, and if you have to wear one of your hats, Mr. Corwin, please make it a small one. They may be on to you by now and we don't want you getting hurt," I warned.

"That's right," Manuel agreed.

"This may be a night I go without a hat. It'll be my undercover look." Corwin sounded far off into his fantasy.

"Let's get back together in two or three days to see what we have, everyone. Be careful, you guys." Manuel was ending the call.

The team agreed and hung up.

I left the office early. I needed air and to get away from the heavy weight of murder for a night. I got home and found myself feeling like a combination target or would-be savior with lingering guilt about my gris-gris doll and Yadira. I knew that I wouldn't really sleep until this case was over. Thankfully, exhaustion ruled and I dozed off until pounding on my door woke me and I sat up straight and scared.

"Dr. Sarah, let me in. Let me in." Fortunately, it was the whiny, copper-tinged voice of Mr. Corwin. I was irritated to be awakened from hard won sleep, but relieved.

"How did you get up here without security calling me?" I asked while I opened the door.

"Remember, you OK'd me the other night? I reminded them of that. I gave them ID, too." He smiled.

I shook my head in frustration. Corwin walked in looking like a true kook. "You're lucky you live in the Bay Area," I said. The remark was lost on him.

"What do you mean?" He had no idea how bizarre he looked.

Corwin wore a classic charcoal-gray Brioni suit, pinstriped and, my guess, about $8,000. But he also wore a burgundy fascinator on his head like those small hats worn by the royal family, cocked to one side with a feather pointed to his right. Despite his oddness, I was eager to hear what he had to say.

"Oh, Dr. Sarah, I'm getting good at this surveillance stuff. I'm learning so much from Mr. Caswell. You know, the techniques are quite interesting…"

"Please, get to the point," I interrupted.

"Well, I went to the Canary Restaurant. Everything is yellow, you know."

I rolled my eyes. Corwin took the hint. "Oh, OK. So I slipped the maître d' a hundred dollars to change their table to one I had hidden my listening device under, and I recorded everything. Don't worry, I didn't wear my hat inside. But I recorded everything!" He was ecstatic.

"Mr. Corwin, you have done a fabulous job." I was proud of my former patient and creepy, crazy person. We listened to the entire recording. It outlined the need to get rid of Yadira but never said who was to do it. Despite that, we decided to play it for the others the next morning. From that point to the end of the case, there were no more secrets among our team. Especially no secrets from Manuel. Before Corwin left, I made a couple of copies of the recording. I wasn't going to take chances with files or information, either. I was too excited to sleep, so I listened to the recordings over and over again to see what else I could learn.

By eleven o'clock the next morning, we were all sitting in a conference room at Manuel's firm, listening to Corwin's recordings:

"I don't want to know details, I just want to know it's all taken care of." It was the voice of Judge Ackers.

"Sure. There are no traces of anything. You-know-who was following her for insurance. She was planning to go to that crazy psychologist bitch and tell her something. We don't know how much she would've told her, but anything would've been risky," Damian said.

Everyone in the conference room looked at me but continued listening.

"Well, the risk was too high. I hope whomever you used was a wise decision?" Judge Ackers asked.

"Totally," Damian assured him. "You wouldn't be surprised. He's your guy." Damian let out a sinister laugh.

"Yep. That's why he's at the meetings. But let's get down to real business," Ackers continued. "What about the shipment? Everything has been on hold for too long. Even with the murder, my contacts are ready to move it or they'll come for all of us."

"Well, we have it rerouted to the pier at Santa Cruz to avoid any interference. I have five guys on it," Damian said.

"I wish we could wait until we get this kid convicted. Yadira's attempt to compromise us and this lengthy case have changed things. Our contacts are nervous. They want to ship and get away from us because they said it seems we have two murders. They want no part of it," Ackers warned. "I really don't understand why you involved those kids in this. It is an unnecessary complication."

"I got Yadira's death ruled an accident, so we're good there. That should help. Don't worry about the rest." Damian said.

"Let's hope. I'll warn you again, nothing and I mean nothing comes to me or is connected to me; is that understood? Remember, my guy is more loyal to me than any of you. He has to be." Judge Ackers warned.

"Yeah. You never let us forget that." Damian answered, coldly. "Keep the money coming, and we're all on the same page." There were sounds of dishes clanging and chairs moving as it seemed the two left the table.

The recording ended. Corwin smiled, proudly.

Manuel's eyes were in tight slits. I now realized that his evil, angry look also meant he had an idea.

"It's time to launch. We have enough now to fuck up their confidence." Manuel smiled.

"What do you mean?" Caswell asked.

"I mean, make the judge think Lis is a risk and make Lis think the judge is high risk. Divide and conquer."

"How in the world do we do that?" The perplexed expression on Jean's face was almost comical.

"We start small fires in many places. Right?" I added. Manuel and I were completing each other's thoughts. "Caswell, leak to your jailer contact that word is Yadira was murdered and there's a secret investigation." I said. Manuel laughed. "That's right, baby, the judge has the most to lose, so he'll be the most nervous and curious about that one—and suspicious of Damian."

"On it," Caswell said.

"At the same time, I'll send a letter to Michael, telling him in his code that there is word out there suspecting the devil made someone do it...or something like that. We need to upset their comfort and get them to turn on each other. We know Michael's mail is being read; that's why I'll use mail rather than a phone call." I was now smiling, wickedly.

"Jean. Get us more on Lis. There has to be more. It might help us to find his hit man or woman." Manuel exhaled. "And more on Yadira's background, too." Jean took notes and shook her head yes.

That moment was magic, almost illuminated. We had a sync-up experience, and we all got it. We left the room and began the execution of our plans to take down a highly connected drug ring and expose a murderer.

CHAPTER THIRTEEN

When you want time to stand still, it won't. Before long, the time had come for Stacy and Lance's god-awful hosted jazz brunch at a small, new restaurant in Berkeley, called Poisson. My analysis was that Stacy had much to prove after being dumped by her husband and nabbing a California doctor helped to sooth her ego about that. I was never quite sure why we humored her. Stacy had no friends in California beyond Lance, so she had pulled from my friends and colleagues for her guest list. Manuel, my motley crew, my girlfriends, and their husbands—all served as Stacy's audience. I had forewarned Manuel it would be a two-martini event.

Three songs in, the band took a break. Lance and Stacy got on stage and walked in lock step to the microphone as if they were hosting the Oscars.

Stacy spoke first. "Everyone, may we have your attention, please."

We all looked around and wondered what was about to happen.

"We know it's only been a couple of months, but we wanted to share our news with all of you first. Lance and I have known each other for just a short time, but we knew from the beginning we were soul mates." Stacy spoke in her fake, breathless voice. Her cohost, Dr. Nerdspeak, was next. "And we are happy to tell you that we are announcing our engagement today. That is the reason we are so extremely pleased you made the time from your busy schedules to attend this brunch. We wanted to make it a surprise, so we did not reveal the engagement. I asked Stacy to marry me after only one month of dating. She makes me feel like I am the only man in the world and the most important man in the world." Lance beamed.

I leaned in to Manuel's ear and whispered, "Sucker…"

"Stop that," he joked.

Nikeba rolled her eyes to the ceiling and motioned for the waiter to pour more wine into her glass. We all laughed. Ma-ma was at a table in front, so she didn't see or hear us. She wouldn't have approved of our cynicism.

Stacy took the mic again and was like the poor man's Marilyn Monroe. "I want all of you to know that when I arrived here in California, I thought that my life was over. I had been hurt so badly. As you know, I wanted to end my life. But so many of you, and especially this wonderful man, came to my aid in helping me to realize there is much more great life to live and great love to live, and I love him so very much. I love you, Lance. Love you, mon cher! *my dear.*" Stacy then blew kisses.

Manuel turned to me with a confused look, "Is he really that blind? She is incredibly fake. Man, some guys just see what they want to see." Manuel shook his head with pity.

I turned and whispered into Manuel's ear, "And what do you see?"

He looked at me intently. "I see that relationships take time, integrity, and trust. Those things don't come with sex, they come with experiences and relating to each other. This is bullshit, but whatever works for them." He ended with an edge to his voice.

"Makes sense," was all I chose to say. I felt it was enough.

After more platitudes, we all danced and mercifully the event ended early. Manuel and I went to his place and enjoyed amazing, liquor-infused sex. He woke up the next morning in a strange mood. "Are you feeling cheated?" he asked as he circled his spoon in blueberry-laced oatmeal. I had inhaled the black coffee.

"What? Where is that coming from?" I asked.

"I know you and your cousin have this competition, and you said she always wins, you end up disappointing your mom and you feel you have to get married. Do you feel cheated with me because I can't commit?" Manuel's eyes had the softness of a baby doe but the intensity of a fox. He couldn't hide years of pain that I knew nothing about.

Love ruled my answer, while I hid my doubts.

"I want what you want. I feel what you feel. I live where you live in this. I want to be in sync with you, not in a contest with my cousin. I want to enjoy a compatible relationship with you, and that's all for now," I said.

Manuel hugged me tightly, and I felt his warm tears trail down my back. In that moment, I didn't give a damn about Stacy or anyone else but I wondered why he even brought it up. An issue without a resolution, I wondered if was I falling too hard, too fast for another disappearing act? *We'll see.*

The following week we began putting our goals into action. We wanted Yadira's murderous drug mob fraying at the edges like a threadbare sweater. With each of our points of contact, we introduced doubt, risk of revelation that would lead to scandal and arrests. Our goal was to loosen the confidence of Damian and his crew so he feared a return to prison, we let the grapevine screw with Ackers fears of being exposed, disbarred and arrested. Our reports back were that they were arguing more and meeting less. But more evidence was needed for the case and we still couldn't identify the killer. I decided to task my gift and to ask for the voice of my late Aunt Cat to bring me deeper wisdom. On that quiet Saturday morning, I put myself into a trance.

"Tante Catin. Je t'aime, tante. *Aunt Catin. I love you, auntie.* How do I solve this? The answers seem so close, but so far," I recited the short question over and over again. Deep within, I heard the precious patois of Aunt Cat.

"Ti-Sarah, Ti-Sarah. It's not so hard, mon cher. Da mind of da wicked is a simple mind, yeah. Dey filled with fear 'cause dey have no faith. Da judge, he fear humiliation and prison. He will do anything to not get caught. Anything. Make him fear getting caught, and he will slip up. Da jailer is plenty evil, cher, murderous evil. He fears prison, too, but more he fears being a poor outcast again. He didn't kill da girl. But you gotta learn to use ya gifts to reveal da whole truth, cher. Dat's da way it gots to be. Dis is a story of da sins of da papa. Da dirty use other hands, but dey are just as guilty, yeah. So proud of you, Ti-Sarah. So proud." Her voice faded.

I sat with that information as I read over notes and my crime kitchen recipe cards. 'Other hands' and 'sins of the father' stayed with me. I hadn't made a connection, but I knew those clues from Aunt Cat would get me to the answers and the murderer. About an hour later my work was interrupted by a call from Jean. "Doctor Sarah, I have new information on Damian Lis. One of the sources I've been hounding sent me an email today. She is kind of not authorized to share this information so she sent it from her home today, rather than her office during the week. You understand."

"I do. That's great she trusted you. What did you find out?" I asked.

"I think I made her feel sorry for Jorge. Anyway, I found out why it was difficult to get into Damian's teen years. It turns out Lis is his alias. His birth name is Damian Kleinhurst."

"Kleinhurst?"

"Yes. And with that name comes a pretty long RAP sheet. He's a big time thief." Jean added. Let me send you this laundry list of his crimes. He moved up from petty crimes to a drug dealing thief. He has done some time, but he must have a great lawyer."

It all began to make more sense. "Or a judge." I offered. Once Jean had given me all of the new insight, I updated my crime kitchen recipe cards and called Manuel.

"I think we need a team meeting at your conference room." I suggested. "We're close to something. I know it." I didn't share Aunt Cat's words because I wanted more time to figure things out myself.

Exotic coffees filled the air in the conference room of Manuel's office. The team, especially Caswell, trailed the pastry filled credenza choosing from muffins, bagels and donuts.

"Everyone. Let's get seated. Jean has important new information to share that could take us closer to cracking this case." I instructed the team while Manuel tapped a pencil on the table. Jean read from her file.

"Good going." Caswell lit up. "He has a record. We can twist him like a twig."

"And tie the judge up in association with a known felon. And how the hell did the jail hire him, even with an alias they should've had better background checks. Great work, Jean." Manuel seemed to presume he was boss now.

"You guys, I think it's time to go in for the kill." I was excited. I could taste success. "Manuel, can you call a meeting with Judge Ackers and use the recording to sweat him out? Or would that violate anything?" I asked.

"Hell no. I want him. And when I say I have recordings, he'll come. He won't talk, but he'll show up." Manuel put his hands together and leaned back in his chair, smiling.

"Caswell, what can you do to our Mr. Kleinhurst to rock his world?"

"I want my clean cop friends to bring him in for questioning for drug smuggling. The recordings give us that." Caswell gave a happy chuckle.

"With all of our surveillance we have recordings and pictures that bring us almost everything but the killer." I said.

"True and I think it gives me reasonable doubt, but I could use more to be sure I can win this. I need one of them to break and reveal who killed Timothy and Yadira." Manuel said. "Let's break them." The team started leaving. I grabbed Jean's elbow and whispered, "Do me a favor."

"Of course." She looked puzzled.

"Now that you have the name, do another pass at Damian's father and family. I'm curious." I said.

"I'm on it." Jean gave a partial smile. And she was on it. Inside of a week we knew more about Damian, the sins of his father and his real life than before.

Setting the traps to break up Yadira's former co-conspirators didn't take long. Later that week, we all met to go over the details and results of the set ups. The odd couple strutted into the office with new confidence, almost cocky. Recent success of our operations had apparently gone to their heads. Caswell's clothes weren't as wrinkled, and he stood straighter and taller. Corwin wore a dark, tailor-made suit. His protective headwear for the day was a black bowler, and were it not for the black panty hose that peeked from under his slacks, he would've looked like a serious businessman instead of...Corwin. I was amused, but it was good to feel we were winning.

"Ok. Let's get this meeting started." Manuel spoke first. I didn't like him taking control of my team, but it was his office. "Under threat of recordings being leaked to the news media, Judge Phillip Ackers met with me. It was a short meeting but it packed a punch. Our conference room supports video recordings." Manuel pointed up to small cameras at the corners of the ceiling. So we listened and watched.

"Before I play this, I assume all of you know I can't use any of these recordings in court but they make powerful leverage." Manuel started the machine.

The attorney for Judge Ackers was a rail of a man who looked like a character out of a British mystery movie. He wore small, round wire-framed glasses that hugged the crevices of his straight nose, and a suit that looked as if it were shipped from London's Savile Row. His name was Bailey. Charleton Bailey.

Once they were all seated, Manuel began with tough questions. "Judge, I'll cut to the chase. We have recordings that prove you are part of a drug smuggling ring. From the recordings, you seem to be doing these deals with a jailer, by the name of Damian Lis. His real name is Damian Kleinhurst. Do you know Mr. Kleinhurst?"

"This is neither a deposition nor hearing, and for that reason, Judge Ackers will not respond to that question." The judge sat with his lips tightly closed. He looked as if he hadn't slept in a few nights.

Manuel continued. "Judge. There is some suspicion that Damian Lis is connected to the murders of Timothy Reston and Yadira Lopez. Do you have any information regarding those murders?"

His attorney again answered. "This is neither a deposition nor hearing and for that reason, Judge Ackers will not respond to that question. He is merely cooperating out of respect to another officer of the court in which there is no ex parte communication because Judge Ackers is not hearing the Timothy Reston case," Bailey recited.

Manuel went through Jean's research, asking the judge about each point of fact in Damian's life. From his parents' divorce, when he was a young boy and his mother's suicide shortly thereafter. He also asked if the judge knew that Damian moved from northern to southern California with his grandparents and fell in with a bad crowd, which resulted in him serving time there. Manuel recited that Damian returned to the Bay Area and allegedly connected with a drug ring. Manuel's last question caused a light wince from the judge, but again, silence. "He served time in the Bay Area and allegedly formed relationships with jailers, dirty cops and you, Judge. Is there any truth to these allegations?" The same response from Bailey.

Predictably, there were no answers from Judge Ackers and after Manuel had completed his list of questions, Ackers and his attorney left.

"Wow." Jean was amazed by the video recording.

"Yeah. He's toast." Caswell said.

"And he knows it. I have to play this the right way so our murder case isn't blown up because of the drug smuggling." Manuel reminded us.

Caswell then gave us the update on his results. "I asked Lis for a clandestine meeting by saying Doc Sarah sent me. I identified myself as a private investigator who might have information he's interested in." Caswell read from his notes.

"I set it up in a parking lot in Oakland. What he didn't know was that I had assembled a team of good cops disguised as delivery truck drivers, cab drivers, homeless people, and pedestrians to surround the parking lot and close in on him."

"Nice." I said.

"He showed up on time. I said, let's talk. I said I have several officers waiting for you to make a wrong move. I would strongly suggest you talk to me," Caswell took a sip of coffee. "I recounted Mr. Kleinhurst's past and he denied it all saying I didn't have proof."

"What happened after that?" Corwin asked.

"I asked him who killed Timothy and Yadira. He said he didn't know and suggested I do something that is anatomically impossible to myself. I lifted my finger and a legion of cops surrounded him." Caswell cocked his head to the side.

"I said to him these good gentlemen will take you in for questioning about both of those deaths. Thank you for your time." I walked away. Corwin gave Caswell a high five.

It was my turn and I gave the update from Michael's set up. "At San Quentin, Michael spread the rumor that the jailers involved with Judge Acker and Damian Lis were at risk because two of them were about to get busted. The result was that one jailer asked to be reassigned, and another flat out quit. Michael had their names and gave them to us. Here they are." I put the list on the table. "I'd say these traps shook up a few rats." I laughed.

"I have something else to share with all of you if you can hang around a bit longer." Manuel raised his voice a little to get our attention. We had started side conversations. "I got a call from my friend Dack Hamilton with DEA. He said they heard about us working on a drug smuggling case involving big names and want to collaborate us."

"How did they hear about us?" I asked.

"Dack said one of Caswell's contacts in the police department told him. I thought that was odd, but maybe they can help. Ironically, it wasn't his idea but his new partner, Reese Thompson. I don't know Reese." Manuel shrugged his shoulders.

"It's not usual for one of my contacts to tell what we're working on. Can I check these guys out?" Caswell asked.

"Sure, they wanted to come by the office today. I arranged it for after our meeting. I didn't want to share recordings or files at this point."

"Good idea." Caswell seemed taken aback. "I wish I coulda had time to run their names past my contacts, but if everyone else is OK, I'm OK." Caswell shrugged his shoulders. I wasn't convinced he was OK with this.

"I wish I would have had vetting time, too. But I'll go with the group." Corwin sat up straight. He was like the kid who says, 'Me, too.'

"I can only vouch for Dack," Manuel reminded everyone. Janelle came to the door. "Your guests are here, Mr. Cabrera."

"Thanks, Janelle. Show them here to the conference room." Janelle returned leading two agents who looked like stereotypes from an action movie. Manuel waved them in. "Oh, come in, you guys." Manuel looked up and said, "Let me introduce you to my team."

That's it. My team is Manuel's team now. Funny how that happened. WTF?

Manuel's possessiveness was met with approval by my now former team, as their chests seemed to puff out a little. I smiled to myself because I was actually glad to see Caswell validated, Jean elevated to work beyond her admin duties, and Corwin part of any group in ways I would have never anticipated. When he used to sit for hours on my therapist's couch, Corwin was incapable of basic social skills. As Aunt Cat used to say, "The Lord works in mystevious"—her word for *mysterious*—"ways." I shelved my ego and let Manuel lead. I raised my head for a closer look at the two tall trees of gorgeous DEA men as they entered the conference room. Manuel's friend, Dack, whom he greeted first, was slender but in shape. He had brown, buzz-cut hair with brown, sparkling eyes. He was a stoically handsome, warrior-looking type. His partner, Reese, who was unknown to Manuel, was the reason I had lost my composure. Not since Manuel had another man caused me to salivate in many places.

"Let me introduce Dack Hamilton, an old friend with the DEA and his partner, Reese Thompson. They have a huge interest in this case."

I handed the two my business cards, although they didn't pass out their cards. Manuel motioned for Dack to speak. He moved to the head of the table and stood. "Thank you, Manuel. We do have a strong interest in this case because of the drug smuggling that happens to involve a suspected drug kingpin whom we have been after for about five years." I wondered if they meant Lis or someone higher.

"My colleague Reese, made us aware of your great investigative work. The alleged involvement of Judge Ackers is a new development."

He turned to Manuel. "Thanks to your team, we have badly needed new leads in this case." He nodded to Reese to speak.

"While the drug deals are our focus, we do hope to help you with your murder case and to solidify the evidence you need. But, I do want to be clear, our priority and jurisdiction has to be the part of the case that involves the drug-smuggling ring."

Caswell looked at me and stretched his eyes as if to say, "I'm not so sure about this." I was in that zone of attraction for the dark-haired Reese Thompson. Although his name didn't suggest it, he had the look of an Irish movie star with intense eyes. He was one of those men whose resting face carried a faint smile, as if he knew a secret you wanted or needed to know.

My physical attraction tell was my inability to sit still and stop crossing my legs, one side to the other when I found myself with the hots. I tried to cover it with a question.

"Just so we're clear, how involved will you be in the investigations of the murders? We need a few more solid pieces of evidence to clear our client." My question seemed redundant and ridiculous. I was ashamed of my obvious attraction to Reese and pitiful attempt to get his attention.

As a brilliant and successful attorney, Manuel had heightened intuition and little got by him. He picked up on my attraction to Reese. I could tell because he refused to hide a glare in my direction. I looked down, pretending to read notes. The meeting evolved into an hour of recap about the case for the two agents. At my direction, each of us shared summaries of what we had learned. We decided not to share the recordings or photographs, though. In turn, it seemed they didn't share much about the drug-smuggling ring. Manuel wrapped up the meeting, retaking charge of the room. Dack and Reese waved good-bye, and an unusual thing happened: Reese stared straight into my eyes and allowed the stare to linger. He wore a serious expression and squeezed his eyes; then he flashed a perfect smile. I always had a weakness for men with intense eyes and magnetic smiles. I was butter, a little heat and I lost all form. They walked out, and everyone looked at me as if I owed them an explanation.

"Wow. When's the date?" Caswell spoke up first.

"I don't think I like that Reese." Corwin used his evil, whiny voice.

Manuel coughed. "Thanks for a great meeting, you guys. I'll keep you posted on Ackers and Lis…or Kleinhurst. Sarah, can you stay for a moment?" he asked. The others left.

Manuel stood over my chair while I looked up at him. "What is up with you?"

"What do you mean?" I asked.

"Sarah. Really?" He cocked his head back.

"Manuel, the man was flirting with me. I didn't do anything," I struggled to camouflage a tiny smile.

"That has nothing to do with my irritation. You are gorgeous; men will flirt with you. That actually makes me proud. My issue is, you showed clear signs of attraction to the man."

My next move caught me off guard because I hadn't planned it. "I love and respect you, but I can't have this conversation right now. I'm going to go to my office." And I got up and walked out. Manuel stood with a slightly opened, silent mouth.

Once back at my desk, Jean walked in. "Whoa, that guy made no secret that he was flirting. That was rude." She shook her head.

"You didn't find it a little sexy?" I asked.

"Oh my God. I give up." Jean looked skyward and left the room.

I pretended to read over notes and review files, but I couldn't stop seeing the gorgeous man with the perfect smile and intrusive eyes.

What the hell is this about?

CHAPTER FOURTEEN

I believe that crazy shit happens in clusters. My badly needed Saturday was interrupted by more crazy. I was at home peering over my crime kitchen recipe cards, which now numbered more than two dozen, when Ma-ma called. My first murder case was coming to a head. I had found myself unwillingly attracted to a new man. I had pissed off the man in my life and heart, but I had to answer Ma-ma's call because...I had to answer.

"Hello?"

"Good morning, Sarah. I hope you weren't busy." Ma-ma had a cheery sound and didn't wait for a response. "I would like your help with something," she declared.

"Well, sure. I do have this case, but tell me what it is, and I'll see what I can do," I said.

"You can imagine how very happy I am for Stacy. It's so good for her to have a second chance." I stifled a giggle.

You mean a fourth. "Sure, Ma-ma. And I'm so glad I was able to introduce her to her next husband." My sarcasm was either ignored or lost on her.

"I would like to begin planning a beautiful engagement party for Stacy. Similar to the beautiful party you had before your engagement turned disastrous. Can you help with the planning for that?" Ma-ma had a gift for flinging a few digs and making questions sound like orders.

"Absolutely." I refused to stoke conflict, but she had pissed me off with that disastrous engagement remark.

"Good, we can start planning. Can you do lunch next weekend?" Ma-ma was closing the deal.

"Sure. Let's meet at Marlin's. Sunday at noon?" I played along. "Do you want me to pick you two up?"

"No, that's OK, cher. We'll have a ride. See you then." Before I could complete a breath to say my next word, she had hung up.

I needed reinforcements, so I called Nikeba.

"Hi, prodigal girlfriend," she answered sarcastically.

"Oh, Nikeba. I've kept you posted on my dealings with the case and Manuel." I chuckled.

"Yes, I love the coded e-mails and text messages. I have Sandy up to speed, too." She said.

"This is an SOS call." I blurted it out.

"Uh-oh. What's happening? Should I conference Sandy in?" She asked.

"May as well, so I can beg once rather than twice."

In a few seconds, Sandy was on the call with us.

"Hi, girls! How's it going?" Sandy sounded as if she had just completed her morning run.

"Hi, Sandy. Catch your breath. I have a huge favor to ask you and Nikeba."

"Great. What? You want us to join the stooges, better known as your team?" Nikeba laughed.

"Nikeba, you can't laugh at them anymore; they've done some good work." Sandy was only slightly serious. "Are you paying Corwin in hats or panty hose?" She joined Nikeba in laughter.

"OK. OK. Enough with the teasing, I have a request worse than becoming part of my comical team."

"Well, go ahead, let it out," Nikeba said.

"Ma-ma wants me to give Stacy a nice engagement party like the one you guys gave me, despite the outcome." I pushed the request out while I still had the guts.

"Oh, hell no. No offense, but your cousin is a grade-A bitch." Nikeba got serious.

"Yeah, Sarah. We went to that jazz brunch announcement thing, but we don't really know her. We did that for you," Sandy agreed with Nikeba.

"I know and I know it's a lot to ask, but you guys love, love planning parties. The fancier, the more expensive, the more fun. And this is a silent nightmare for me. Remember, Lance was a one-night stand who dumped me, and even though I'm with Manuel now, it's still awkward. I can't get out of this. Please, please, please…" I whined.

"Jesus. You're pathetic when you're begging. I like smartass-cocky Sarah better," Nikeba snarked.

"Me, too. You need a drink." Sandy teased. "But we do give a helluva party. Nikeba, she sounds so pitiful, let's help. To hell with Stacy. I vote we do this. I think we'll get some laughs out of it. Stacy is like a caricature." Sandy chuckled.

"Yeah, she does bring that Louisiana crazy into a room." Nikeba had changed her mind, as well. "We'll give that slut a party. No offense."

"Oh please. I'm not emotionally connected to this or Stacy," I clarified. "And to put all the cards on the table, Ma-ma wants to do an organizing meeting, noon next Sunday at Marlin's. Can you guys make it? Martinis on me after the meeting."

"Hell, I'll need to drink *through* the meeting. I can be there." Nikeba had a smile in her voice.

"Me, too. Gotta go now, but see you guys next week." Sandy was signing off.

"I love you chicks!" I yelled into the phone.

"Don't call us chicks, broad. Girl, bye." Nikeba laughed loudly, and we all hung up.

Manuel and I were still Ok, but had no weekend plans because he wanted to work Saturday and Sunday. I didn't expect any more calls from Ma-ma, because she had her way. My motley crew didn't seem to need anything from me, so when my mobile phone rang a few hours later, I wondered who was attached to the unfamiliar number.

"Hello?"

"Hi, Dr. Jean-Louis. I hope that I'm not intruding by calling you on a Saturday." A sturdy, sexy voice flowed through the phone. "This is agent Thompson. Reese. We met at Manuel Cabrera's office."

"Oh yes. How are you, Agent Thompson?" I felt my stomach flutter.

"Call me Reese, please," he said. "I'm doing well, but I have some information that you might want. I wasn't able to get in touch with Manuel. Are you free for a quick coffee or a drink around five today? I hate to hold on to this information."

"Oh, um, please call me Sarah. Well, I didn't really have plans today. I can assemble the team…"

Reese interrupted. "No, no need to gather the entire group. It'll be faster to meet with you and you can fill them in."

"Um, OK. Not a problem. Can you meet in Oakland? How about The Diner downtown?" I chose a familiar place.

"Sure. I'll see you at five." He hung up.

The truth was, it was an ego rush for the handsome agent to flirt with me, and I assumed he had made up an excuse to see me. My intuitive wisdom and inner voices blared, 'don't go,' but ego won out. I had at least two hours before it was time to shower and dress, so I resumed my review of case information and poured myself a glass of wine. It was a moment that would change everything. As I pulled the photos closer to my face, all I needed to know jumped out at me from the pictures. I finally realized where I had seen Damian Lis's familiar, distinguishing jawline; it was nearly identical to the jawline of Timothy Reston from the ME's photos of his body. I knew it couldn't be a coincidence. I wondered if Damian had fathered Yadira's biological son, Timothy. The sins of the father began to manifest. I ignored the ring of my cell phone for two reasons; I finally had a breakthrough on my clues from Aunt Cat and, because it was Manuel's number and I sure as hell didn't want to tell him I was going to meet with Reese.

I closed my eyes to see what the photos of Damian and Timothy would inspire. Visions came in like a flood with flu symptoms. I saw the older man with Yadira in labor again. This time I saw his face. He had the same jawline and was like an older version of Damian. As in the earlier vision he got up and left. As I swallowed hard to fight a feeling of fever and chills, I then saw Judge Ackers and Reese. I didn't think they knew each other. In the vision, Reese seemed subservient as if taking orders from the judge. That scene faded and then

Reese appeared standing in a dark place wearing black gloves and dark glasses. *Oh my God! Reese is somehow involved in the murder case!* I squeezed my eyes tighter shut in a failed attempt to extend the vision and learn more. My hands shook as I took a sip of wine. *No wonder he asked Dack to contact Manuel about the case. He is involved. He has a role in this. Caswell was on to something, it didn't make sense that one of his contacts would tell Reese or anyone at DEA what we were working on. Reese knows about us because of the judge. Holy Shit!* My stomach turned as I came to the realization about Reese. I poured over our photos and the dark suit guy whose face never showed up. I knew now that he had Reese's build. In one that showed him in profile, he wore a dark suit and dark glasses. I thought about the man with the dark glasses and fake beard and who tried to kill Manuel. I shivered with the thought that I was to meet with Reese. I had little over an hour to figure out what to do. I decided to meet Reese because after all, I'd be in my own car and in a public place. Maybe I could find out something from him. I showered and dressed without regard for fashion. My attraction for Reese had ended abruptly. *All I want now is to solve the case and get that band of rats arrested.*

My phone rang again while I was in the shower. I checked the number and it was Manuel calling for a second time. I didn't call him back. I continued to dress for my meeting with Reese, green sweater, black skinny pants with black flats. My hands shook too much to put on any jewelry. I walked out of my front door and went down the elevator to the parking garage. I looked down at my phone and noticed another call from Manuel. As I was about to open my car door, one swish of a movement blinded me, I was grabbed and shoved facedown onto the backseat of another car. My phone had dropped to the garage floor. I was powerless and scared to death, with a scarf tied tightly over my eyes, a gag around my mouth, and my hands tied behind my back. A harsh reminder to always obey my inner voice.

"Humph, mmmmm, mmmm." I made a futile attempt to protest and fight back. My sounds were muffled, and my wiggling had accomplished nothing.

I wondered who had done this to me. The man's voice was familiar, but now scary. "Sorry Sarah, you won't make it to The Diner. You have plans." It was unmistakably Reese. My heart raced in fear. I could feel my tears as I wept uncontrollably. I regretted not listening to my intuitive voices. In my mind, I spoke to the spirit of Aunt Cat and told her I was on the way to see her again, this time in the nonphysical. I knew now that Reese was a killer. He may have killed Yadira and Timothy and I would be next.

"Sarah, you have to understand." Reese talked as he drove. The feel and sounds of the road led me to believe I knew the route. I thought we were headed for the Bay Bridge, maybe even the road near the toll bridge where Yadira had met her end. Reese kept talking. "This is not personal. I get paid to perform these assignments. You were on my client's list, so I got Dack to involve us in the case. I don't have anything against you, I have to do what my clients pay me to do. You and that ratty little team kept getting too close to the facts and made them nervous, so we need to exterminate the leader. I'm sure you understand. But then again, it doesn't matter if you don't." Reese then hissed loud, psychotic laughter, the same laughter I had heard in one of my scariest visions. The rest of the ride, he was quiet.

After what seemed like a lifetime on my stomach in the back seat of Reese's car, we stopped. I felt the car move from the freeway to the rugged service road. I knew it well. I could hear waves crashing against the rocks. In the next moments, I wondered if I would be drugged or just tossed into the Bay, tied up and unable to swim. I wondered if I would be shot. My mind raced, cloudy with fear and panic. And all at once, I accepted my end. I accepted my stupidity and naïveté. I accepted I had reached the end of my life, murdered. I would be the next case to solve. I heard my captor get out of the car. He lifted me from the back seat and I was forced to walk a short distance across the rocks. We went inside of a building and I was tied to a chair and a door slammed. I strained to listen to a conversation in the next room. I heard voices, Reese and the other was without a doubt the voice of Judge Ackers. I knew it from hours of recordings from Corwin and Manuel.

"Before we dump her in the Bay, I want to know what she knows." Ackers said. "You can't kill all of them, so let's get the information I'll need to clear myself before we take her down."

"Sure. I can make her talk." Reese chuckled.

"First, let's see if she'll cooperate. Let's go in." Ackers said.

The men didn't remove my blindfold, but pulled the gag from my mouth. Ackers spoke first. "I'll tell you right now, screaming will do no good. No one will hear you out here."

"I know, Judge Ackers. I'm in the same place you got rid of Yadira." I tried to sound tough.

I could feel that both were startled. "What do you know about Yadira's death?" he asked.

"I know it wasn't an accident. I saw that Hummer run her over. I wonder who was driving. You Judge, or you, Reese?" I taunted. I felt the sharp pain of a thick hand across my face. "You shut the fuck up, you crazy bitch." Reese slapped me with the power of a freight train. My face stung so hard I tasted blood in my mouth.

The judge yelled at him. "Stop it. I need to get more information from her, you idiot. What she knows, the rest of them know. Now, you talk or there's more of that for you." Ackers ordered.

"Judge, I know that you got suckered in this one." As I spoke, the words came spilling from my mouth as if someone or something had power over them. I said things I had no way of knowing. "Damian used you to get his own revenge, that's why you will be tied to two murders." My voice had taken on a sinister quality.

"What do you mean? What revenge." He sounded desperate.

"That kid had nothing to do with you. He was a snitch, but he was Damian's brother and Yadira's son by Damian's father. He fooled Yadira into killing the boy to get revenge on her for having an affair with his father. His mother committed suicide because of it. He brought that shit into your drug deal." I kept talking and then, magically, I began to quote the judge from one of our recordings. "Oh, that's fucking great. A jailhouse, connected snitch bunked up with your step kid, sharing a space, likely talked his goddamn head off. Now he turns up dead, and you believe someone won't connect that to you and us? What kind of fucked-up lawyer are you? And whatever harebrained strategy this was supposed to be has just put all of us at risk. This operation now has lines to all of us."

"Goddamn it. She was in on the recordings that lawyer Manuel told us about. Son of a bitch. We are all recorded by this group of rank amateurs." Ackers began to yell. "What have you done with those tapes? Who has them? You better tell me in the next two minutes!"

I continued. "And did you know that Reese tried to kill Manuel, I guess on your orders." I could tell I had them freaked out.

"What the fuck did you do?" The judge asked Reese.

"But you said we needed to take care of them." Reese answered.

"Oh, hell. You fucking loser. You are all losers. Because of all of you, I might go to prison whether you kill this scary bitch or not. They have recorded us and we are fucked." I heard the judge shove a chair.

"Look Judge, I'm not going down for this, I . . . .ooh." Reese pushed out a grunt. I heard rushing and more footsteps. Then I heard the Judge Ackers surrender. "OK. OK. I'm not armed. I'm not armed."

"Sarah. You OK?" It was the voice of Caswell. The beautiful, awkward New Jersey accent of Caswell. Tears streamed my face in relief.

Then I heard the copper-tinged, whiny sing-song of Mr. Corwin. Crazy, awesome, stalking Mr. Corwin. I was overcome with disbelief and gratitude. He and Caswell had saved my life. I wept nonstop as they untied my hands and removed the blindfold. I stood up and hugged my crew, my awesome crew. I didn't want to let go of them. I saw Reese and Judge Ackers being led away in handcuffs by Oakland Police. I cried uncontrollably as I released the terror and fear that I hid while held captive.

"It's OK now, Doc Sarah. You're with us and you're all right." Caswell's avuncular tone helped to slow my heaving chest. Corwin's comfort came from a different place. "Dr. Sarah, I wanted to kill him, but Caswell insisted we include the police. I didn't like him when I met him. And I thought he looked familiar, like part of that crooked group, but it wasn't obvious because he was always the guy I couldn't identify who wore dark glasses and was never called by a name. How dare he try to kill you." Corwin turned and yelled to Reese as he was being guided into the police car. "You bitch!"

"Calm down, Corwin. We got her. We got her." I heard the effort to conceal tears in Caswell's voice. The two held me up, and we walked to Caswell's car. I got into the backseat and thanked all of my spirit guides for putting the words in my mouth to shock those crooks and save my life. One of the police officers made way to the car and asked Caswell if I was able to give a statement.

"Doc Sarah, can you tell the officer the basics so they can book these jackasses?" Caswell asked.

"Yeah, I can do that." I answered weakly. I repeated the series of events about three or four times as the officer took my statement. Each time, new tears creased my face and traced the lines around my mouth. I didn't tell them how I taunted the two with details of the killings of Yadira and Timothy. I stuck to the kidnapping and attempted murder of me.

"Thank you, miss. That's enough for now. We'll want to speak with you again later."

"I understand. I'll be available," I replied, softly.

Once the officer was out of sight, Caswell handed me a flask filled with vodka. I took two large gulps.

"Ahh. Thank you. You two saved my life. My life." My voice quivered as I spoke. "You saved me."

"Doc Sarah, it's part of our job. You're so good to us. We will always protect you." Caswell swallowed hard and drew in a sniffle. He looked at me from the rearview mirror as he drove. Corwin was in the passenger seat, dabbing his eyes with his handkerchief.

"Yes. Dr. Sarah, you have given me a new life. I'll protect you. I will." Corwin then continued to sniffle and weep softly. He was wearing a tan English driving hat.

After a few more vodka gulps, I was ready to talk. "How in the world did you guys know where to find me? How did you know about Reese?"

"Ya see, Manuel had been trying to contact you, and when you never answered or called back, he got worried and contacted us. He's headed to your place now, by the way. Corwin here has been keeping an eye on your building almost all the time, so when I told him that Manuel was worried when you didn't answer your phone, he told me to get over there," Caswell explained.

"That's right. There's been too much going on with this case to take a chance. I saw Reese come to your place, and I thought it was just a date, but I still didn't trust him. When his car rushed out of your garage, and we didn't see your head, we looked in the garage for you." Corwin nodded.

Caswell shook his right index finger into empty space. "We found your cell phone on the garage floor and knew that wasn't good. Fortunately, getting out of your garage takes some time, and we were able to follow him. We saw him take you into that old building at the side of the Bay Bridge by the toll booths." Caswell explained.

"We were watching through the windows." Corwin said.

"I had called my cop friends and they asked me not to try to take Reese by myself. I had my hand on my Glock and almost used it when he slapped you. But when they kept you talking, I gave the cops a few more minutes. I had a sight on Reese and was ready to drop him." Anger had returned to Caswell's voice.

I pushed out a deep breath. "Oh, thank God." The vodka had made its presence impossible to ignore. "Thank you, everybody." My voice trailed off. I wasn't sleepy, just tipsy and exhausted.

"We're here," Caswell announced into his cell phone. "Yeah, we got her, and we're in front of her place, parking the car." He hung up. "That was Manuel, he'll be here in a few minutes. He's on the way."

Caswell clapped his newish, old-school flip phone shut. We went up to my place. It felt like a warm, secure cocoon. I collapsed on my sofa. Despite security's call to allow Manuel up, his forceful knock at the door startled me.

"It's me." Manuel spoke through the closed door. Caswell let him in and he ran to me. We hugged. It was clear that we didn't want to let go. We kissed in front of the guys for the first time. The danger had changed us. Manuel pulled back and noticed my bruised and swollen face. "Oh my God. They hit you?" Manuel's jaw tightened.

"It was bad, but that was all." I assured him. He looked to Caswell.

"I was gonna rush the bum with my gun, but PD didn't want me to act alone. Trust me, Manuel. If he would've tried anything after that, I had a sightline on him to blow his head off." Manuel nodded approval. By the time Jean arrived, I had calmed enough to offer everyone wine and snacks. Manuel served. Jean dabbed at my face with an ice pack. I repeated my story to the group at least as many times as I had done for the police officer at the scene. But I shared more with the team. I had an important fact that my gut told me to keep from the police officer.

"Before I left to meet Reese, I was able to put clues together and with visions, figure out who killed Timothy and Yadira. That information saved my life because the judge wanted to know how much we all knew. He kept Reese at bay." I stopped to take in a deep breath.

"I recognized the unmistakeable resemblance Timothy had to Damian. My visions revealed the rest and I used that information to upset Judge Ackers."

"How did you do that," Jean asked.

"I told him Damian used his drug deal to get revenge on Yadira and to support his manipulation of her. He got her to kill her own biological son. He made Yadira and the judge believe Timothy had told Jorge about them so Timothy had to be killed and Jorge convicted of the murder."

"That calculated bastard." Manuel said. "We made sure they picked him up before he could run."

"Good thing." I affirmed.

"And that son of a bitch, Reese is a hit man doubling as DEA. Well, he's done now." Caswell shook his head.

"There all done. I'll make sure of it." Manuel's eyes twinkled with a deadly anger.

CHAPTER -FIFTEEN

"**W**hat about a theme, like birds or angels?" Ma-ma pretended to place party planning in our hands but all the while she attempted to control the entire event for Stacy and Lance. Control was her signature. I hadn't shared my kidnapping ordeal with Ma-ma or the girls. The DA held the story until charges could be filed. With a judge involved they handled the case carefully. I had the luxury of a few days before the entire story would become public.

"Themes are great. We would have to fully integrate the theme into other aspects of the party, so let's explore some ideas, soup to nuts." Nikeba was unusually diplomatic as she treated Ma-ma gently.

As if noticing me for the first time, Nikeba gawked. "Sarah, what the hell happened to your face?"

"I had a little car accident riding with one of the guys. I'm fine, though. It's getting better." I said.

"I didn't want to say anything, but I was hoping no one had hit you." Ma-ma frowned.

"If by no one you mean Manuel, forget it. He wouldn't hit me." I rolled my eyes in frustration. Before I furthered the point, I felt the presence of evil, and then a flat, accent-laden familiar voice invaded our planning meeting from the women's restroom.

"Hi, y'all!" Stacy walked toward us wearing jeans so tight the seams stretched for dear life, five-inch heels, and a tight red shirt that had a peek-a-boo hole to her cleavage. "I'm so grateful that y'all are planning a party to celebrate my engagement. And thank you, Aunt Bernice, for making this possible." She hugged Ma-ma as my stomach flipped.

In response to the startled expressions of Nikeba and Sandy, Ma-ma explained. "Didn't Sarah tell you that Stacy would be here? I thought that since the party's not a surprise, you could ask for her input." Ma-ma smiled. I was amazed at Ma-ma's talent for denial. Stacy gave me a victorious, sly smile and winked. I knew all too well what it meant. She would wink at me when she felt she had the upper hand or had sufficiently humiliated me. "Oh my God, Sarah. Who hit you? That's a nasty looking bump, cher."

I answered quickly and moved on. "Car accident. Thanks for asking. Let's make good use of this time." I kept focused.

Nikeba was quick on her feet. "Well Stacy, let's talk about themes for the party. What do you like?" she asked.

"Um, what do you mean?" Stacy asked softly in her whisper voice.

"Do you like a certain flower, or color, or item? Do you have any hobbies, interests, symbols that you are known for? We can design the party around them." Nikeba was politely impatient.

"Uhhhhh. I don't know. Let me think." Stacy put her right index finger onto her mouth while she—allegedly—thought. It's amazing how the human body can hold high levels of stupidity without strain. And in a response that should've embarrassed my entire lineage, my whore-bitch cousin responded with, "Well, I like desserts." That was followed with a clueless smile under blank eyes.

Sandy, who was now two mimosas in, laughed out loud. Ma-ma could barely conceal her embarrassment. Nikeba breathed out obvious frustration, and I grabbed the moment for quick ego relief. "No, Stacy. They need to work with themes. You *do* know what themes are; right?"

"I do know what themes mean, Sarah; you don't have to talk down to me," Stacy shot back to me. Sexy, whisper voice had now gone.

"Well, if I talk up to you, you won't be able to understand me." I returned the volley, satisfied.

"Girls, girls. Let's not have this." Ma-ma raised her voice.

I had postured for rebuttal. Stacy had verbally reloaded.

She leaned into my direction, venomous. "Look, Sarah. I may not have your education, but I have what you'll never have: sex appeal and the ability to get a man. You're just jealous 'cause Lance dumped you last year. Yeah, he told me all about it, Ti-Sarah." Stacy paused to catch her breath. She looked satisfied from her narrative.

My mouth opened in disbelief. Stacy's attack was unnecessarily cruel and out of place. It seemed to have been fueled by decades of resentment. My girls and Ma-ma stared at Stacy with disapproval.

"Girls, girls, let's not argue in public." Ma-ma pleaded.

But in the company of a nemesis, reason doesn't always win out. So, I went there...I wasn't loud or overly angry, I was on point.

"Look you crazy, ignorant, aging sex kitten. If you haven't noticed, Manuel is the perfect man to make a woman forget there ever was a... what's his name? Lance?" I warmed up. "And you don't have anything I want. So shut up. Be grateful I could talk these two busy women into doing a party to honor this farce." I raised my voice.

Ma-ma stood up, angry and indignant. "Sarah! How dare you!" Ma-ma began, but I had a vodka-soaked throat and forty years of frustration to accompany it.

"How dare I what? Put up with a mother who constantly criticizes me because my success threatens her Creole code? How dare I call out a fake engagement by a woman who resents me and uses her body as currency? Or maybe, how dare I say, enough of this being used. Nikeba, Sandy, you are my friends, and you don't have to be pulled into this nonsense." I gulped more drink and blinked.

To my surprise, neither Ma-ma nor Stacy rebutted. My rant had apparently reached a truth-nerve within them, or they needed the help and my money so they played along. Either way, their responses shocked me and the girls.

"I'm sorry, Sarah. I don't mean to be mean to you." Ma-ma held her head down and asked for a glass of vodka. For the first time in forever, I saw my petite, proper Ma-ma chug a vodka neat with a water back.

Stacy tried too hard. "Oh, Ti-Sarah, I was outta line, yeah. Please forgive me, and I need your help, y'all. All of y'all. I ask that you please don't leave me alone with this and that you help me to have a party. I'm really trying to be a better person. I know I blow up and insult you,

Sarah, but I apologize. If nothing else, can't we have a fun party that everybody can enjoy?" Stacy looked at me with a bashful smile.

"Nikeba and Sandy, it's up to you. Do you want to take on this dysfunctional family for a party?" I asked.

"We all have family. I'm in if Sandy is. We do love throwing parties." Nikeba let a smile break through her serious face. Sandy nodded in agreement. We poured drinks, liberally, and toasted every and any thought or notion. In the midst of it, I knew that Ma-ma was having a breakthrough and finding herself, separate from the memory of our father. She became tipsy but enjoyed the freedom to drink and laugh with us. I also knew that Stacy remained a phony. I could see in her eyes that resentment of me would remain after this party and throughout our lives. She had no love for Lance or anyone; she could only love Stacy. I also knew that I would have to keep an eye on her forever. She was in California now to stay, and she would take any opportunity to hurt me. It appeared to be her mission.

As if she heard my thoughts, Stacy flashed an overdone smile in my direction. And I saw the smile transition into a straight, harsh face. I could tell that Stacy's mischief had only begun.

CHAPTER -SIXTEEN

The next day brought poetic justice. Once we had handed over Jean's extensive research, Corwin's recordings and photos, and my crime kitchen recipe cards, (they laughed at those), the police had the information they used for leverage to cut deals in the murders of Timothy Reston and Yadira Lopez. It was my first time using my visions to solve a crime and I was excited. Manuel had prepared me and my team to testify as the case was made. We were ready to celebrate our first victory.

"Damian was eager to cut a deal. He gave up Reese, the judge and everybody involved." Manuel explained.

I invited Nikeba, Steve, Sandy and Raphael to join my team for celebratory drinks at my place so they could hear all of the details.

"We heard from a few of our contacts that you guys are credited with enabling the DA's office to make the case. I never would've believed it." Nikeba chuckled.

"We have to hear this story in its entirety Sarah." Sandy nudged.

"We did some good work." Jean said.

"I'll use these cards to explain each person's role in this horrendous crime and why the real killer will be charged and Jorge set free." I said.

"Are those your personalized recipe cards?" Nikeba asked with a snicker.

"Yes. But forget about that." I laughed. "We have to go back twenty years ago and use Jean's great research," I began. "A young Yadira was a student having an affair with a professor at Cal State East Bay. She became pregnant and that child was Timothy Reston. "Whoa." Sandy was surprised.

"We later learned that the professor who was Timothy's father was also the father of Damian Lis or Kleinhurst, Damian's real name.

Nikeba's husband, Steve spoke up. "Damn." He looked at Raphael, Sandy's husband, who said, "this is crazy, like a movie."

I kept going. I enjoyed having the floor. "Exactly. I had noticed from the photos Lis's unique jawline was the same as Timothy's. At first I thought Damian might've been his father, but taking into account timeframes and locations, that wasn't likely."

"That's brilliant, Sarah." Nikeba marveled.

"Thanks. Damian's father wanted to marry Yadira, but she wanted to go to law school and get rich. She had struggled as a child and wanted no part of marrying an older man or becoming a mother. She had been hardened by her tough life. Professor Kleinhurst, Damian's father, had fallen in love with her and had asked his wife for a divorce. He told his wife about Yadira and the pregnancy," I continued.

"The problem was he told his wife about the pregnancy before he realized Yadira would refuse to marry him." Manuel added to the story. "She planned to give the baby up for adoption and go on with her life."

"That's right. But by then it had exploded. The mother committed suicide and Damian blamed Yadira for that. His father lost his job and was ruined. Damian was sent to live with his grandparents in Southern California and fell in with a bad crowd." I taped the Damian crime kitchen recipe cards on my wall and connected them to Yadira, his father and Timothy.

Caswell picked up the next part of the story. "Damian wanted revenge. Even though he was in southern California he had kept up with Yadira's life. He had also become involved in the drug world. When he heard Yadira was an attorney, he decided to contact her and figure out a way to ruin her." Caswell made his signature circular motions with his right hand.-

"But how could he do that? She was an attorney." Nikeba asked.

"He used a fake name when he came back up to NorCal and seduced Yadira. She had never met Damian when she was sneaking around with his dad. He told police he could tell she would do anything for money. He eventually told her about the smuggling ring and that they had cops and a judge involved for their protection," I answered.

"Ah, so she jumped on the opportunity." Sandy pulled it all together.

"Exactly," I added.

"So what about Timothy? Where does that come in?" She asked.

"Yadira did put him up for adoption. She never saw the baby after the day he was born. Unfortunately, he had a horrible childhood in foster homes and eventually a home with abusive parents. Yadira married an innocent widower with a son. She hated the son and wasn't really in love with the dad. She began having the affair with Damian while married. They divorced, but she had done damage to Jorge by then. She was the evil stepmother for sure," Manuel explained. "I didn't know any of this before this case, despite knowing Yadira for many years. You never know what's going on in someone else's home." Manuel shook his head.

"That's true for sure. Damian confessed to police that he used his connections to get Timothy and Jorge thrown into the same cell. That gave him opportunity. He lied to Yadira and told her that Timothy knew about the drug ring and had told Jorge about it while they were in jail together. In his confession, Damian said he made it possible for Yadira to get into the jail and inject Timothy with potassium chloride. Yadira unknowingly killed her own biological son."

"Damn, he concocted a helluva plot." Nikeba said.

"Yep, he's the face of evil. He even told the DA it was his idea for Yadira to work for Manuel and use his law firm in Jorge's case." I explained. Manuel's eyes tightened at the mention of that part of the story.

"Damien bragged to Yadira about his manipulation of her. Once Yadira found out she had been tricked into murdering her son, she contacted me. They had been following her and the judge hired Reese to kill her." I swallowed. "And me, as it turns out." I added a note about the Yadira meeting under her crime kitchen recipe cards.

"My job has definitely been easier because of all of you. You're a great team, and you guys have done a fantastic job. Each and every one of you." Manuel looked around the room.

Corwin looked down, proudly and moved his orange, floppy-brimmed straw hat out of his eyes. I looked around the room at the unlikely individuals who had become a sharp team of investigators. I quietly thanked Aunt Cat and my spirit guides for clues to the murders, as the sins of the father and the use of other hands all came together.

"Ok. Let's get on to the next one." Jean's enthusiasm made us laugh.

"Hold on." Manuel laughed. "First, let's toast. I brought champagne for Mr. Corwin and everybody."

I looked with pride at the team I had created. I would send Michael a thank you for his role. And I laughed to myself knowing I had found the work I was truly meant to do.

"Oh look," Jean stood up. "Let's turn up the TV, there's Manuel on the news."

Manuel and the district attorney dominated local news for nearly a week as they were interviewed about details of Judge Ackers, Reese, and Damian Lis. Jorge was freed and video of his father crying and hugging him touched us all.

"Sarah, I have to eat crow." Nikeba laughed as we clicked our champagne glasses.

"Oh you of little to no faith." I laughed.

"Yep. You guys pulled it off." Sandy raised her glass.

"Sarah, one day I want to learn some spells or chants or some of that Creole spirit shit. It works for you," Nikeba teased.

"Yeah, it does. I'm not sure what's next, but the spirits will move me," I joked in a spooky voice.

"What's next is your cousin's engagement party. And if I may say so, Nikeba and I have outdone ourselves with this one," Sandy added.

"Oh, don't remind me," I moaned. "But I can't wait to see how you transformed that idiot's ideas into a cool party."

"It was a challenge, because she's lazy. Frankly, I think she was glad that we took it over." Nikeba sipped. "And we expect to see all of you at this engagement party. Misery loves company." She announced.

"Well, I better call it a night. I need some rest." Caswell stood up and motioned for Corwin to join him toward the door.

"Same here." Sandy added. She, Raphael, Nikeba and Steve also stood and kissed me goodbye. Jean followed them all out.

I turned to Manuel who was sitting on the sofa. "You look so good on TV. But, you look better in person." I sat next to him and pulled his arm around my shoulders.

"Thank you. How about I stay here tonight and we continue celebrating?" He asked.

"Now that's one of your better ideas."

Epilogue

The weeks following the successful end of the Jorge Lopez case delivered us to the date of Stacy and Lance's engagement party. I opened my door to Manuel. He looked like a tall, gorgeous prince. He wore a Zegna suit in navy pinstripe with a royal blue tie, pale blue shirt, and chocolate lace-up shoes that looked like Ferragamos. "Are you ready for this?" he asked as I stood admiring him.

"Always." I leaned in and kissed him on the cheek.

"That's not the 'this' I meant, but that's pretty good." He laughed.

"I know. I have to watch Stacy take center stage and listen to the unspoken bitch code she uses with me." I motioned for Manuel to come inside. "I'll get my purse, just a minute."

"Wait a minute. Sarah, she's no one for you to feel inferior to any longer. She's not you by any stretch. She's actually pretty pathetic. You might feel sorry for her," Manuel encouraged.

"Yeah. I'm trying to get there. I want to tell you something and I hope you don't think less of me, but I have to get it out in the open with you," I said.

Manuel's brow spiked. "What is it? Something bad?"

"Kind of." I kept my head down. I couldn't look at him during my confession. "Last year, I had a one-night stand with Lance. I had too much to drink and didn't realize it until morning. He dumped me after that. But you remember how he helped during Michael's case. He wanted to begin going out again, but I was too attracted to you to accept. When he met Stacy he went gaga for her." I looked up.

Manuel gave a quiet chuckle.

"Why is that funny?" I was confused.

"Sarah, I figured it was something like that, last year. I knew you had either dated or had a thing. I was going to go for you no matter what. I knew I could get you from him. Nice guy but dull as paste." He laughed.

"But…" I started.

"But nothing. We all have past lives and past loves. Let's keep them in the past." Manuel kissed me and motioned for me to go get my purse. "I even. . . .nah, let's not do this." Manuel seemed primed for a confession of his own, but he stopped. My intuition knew it was Yadira, but I didn't press him.

"Let's get this shit over with." He smiled.

I looked to the ceiling and mouthed a thank you as I picked up my purse off the bed and rushed to the living room. We left for the party, not knowing what to expect from the bizarre duo of Stacy and Lance.

When Manuel drove up to the valet service at the historical Oakland History Gallery, I could tell that Nikeba and Sandy had outdone themselves again. We walked into a room with hints of gold and emerald green in flowers and lights. The twenty-foot-high, five-thousand-square-foot elliptical dome gave a royal atmosphere to the party. Columns and gold trim made the place glow with elegance. Soft, smooth jazz played in the background, and Nikeba instructed Lance and Stacy to greet guests as they entered.

"Oh, Sarah, this is like a fairy tale." Stacy kissed my cheeks and hugged me hello.

"It sure is," I agreed with a double entendre. *This is a tale of some sort.*

"Sarah, you look lovely. It is wonderful to see you and Manuel." Lance beamed.

The drinks being passed included champagne with flecks of gold inside, and green colored Hurricanes, the lethal drink created in New Orleans. Ma-ma greeted guests and served in the role that would traditionally had been held by Stacy's mother, my late Aunt Cat. My siblings and their families mingled with Lance's family and scores of friends. Dozens of relatives like Stacy's sisters and brothers had come to the party from Louisiana. Cousins, nieces, nephews and a few surviving aunts and uncles, filled the tables reserved for family. The invitations explained that the couple would have a destination wedding in the Carribbean and not a local ceremony, so the engagement party served as the event for family and friends to enjoy.

"Hi guys." I walked over to Caswell and Corwin, who now hung out together like good friends. Caswell was drinking Hurricanes. He was in a dark dress suit. It wasn't expensive or pressed well, but he looked good.

"This is OK stuff," Caswell said. "I usually go for whiskey neat, but this is good."

"Be careful with those Hurricanes. They hit you hard, like a storm. You'll love them," I joked.

"I'm fine with the champagne." Corwin spoke from behind the white veil of his pillbox hat. He wore a dark suit and black dress shoes to complete his look.

Stacy and Lance stopped the band to address the guests, but I never heard their speeches. Manuel had motioned for me to follow him into a hallway that bordered the main room.

"Sarah, I wanted this night to be special for you and me too," Manuel began.

"Every night with you is special. I'm fine. I'm good now that we've talked and everything is on the table," I said.

"That's not what I mean." Manuel struggled, uncharacteristically with his words.

"I don't understand."

"I have a bulge in my pants for a reason." Manuel smiled.

"Oh my God, I'm not going to do that here. That's so wrong." I frowned.

"Not that." He laughed. "This." Manuel pulled a ring box from his pants pocket and opened it.

"Oh my God! Oh my God! Is that...?" I was shocked. It was the last thing I expected.

"It's a ring. Sarah. I don't know when or if I want to get married, but if you'll promise to give me some time to work on myself, I promise

I will try commitment to you. I'm giving you this ring to say, when I figure it out, I want it to be you." Manuel spoke slowly.

"This is such an incredible surprise. I'm speechless." My mouth spoke the words, while my heart held slight resentment. It was a compliment and an insult rolled into one. To learn that the man you love is not sure he can commit to you, but if he decides to commit, it'll be you is no great honor. So, take this ring and wait around in case I decide I want to marry you. *WTF is that? I won't blow the moment, but this is not as great as he thinks it is.*

"Well, at least answer the question," he insisted.

"What's the question?" I asked playfully.

"Will you be my fiancée? And one day, wife?" Manuel asked.

The sting of the iffiness fell awkwardly on my ear. I loved him, but I had no idea what this almost-proposal really meant. Despite that, I accepted.

"I will be your fiancée, one day wife," I agreed.

Manuel smiled and put a beautiful ring of emerald surrounded in diamond baguettes on my finger. It fit perfectly. The backdrop of the party had disappeared. I wasn't sure what the future would bring, but I knew I had stepped into a new journey with this unpredictable man. As I hugged Manuel, I caught a glimpse of Stacy looking directly at me with hateful, snake eyes. She seemed to have Yadira's evil glances now. She had been watching us and I could tell she saw Manuel give me the ring. I thought to myself, *Whatever the future brings, I will not let your ass make me feel unworthy or unattractive again.* And this time, I gave the confident, victorious wink to her. Stacy quickly turned her head away. I realized that no matter how many murder cases I would work on in the future with my team, I would also have to work at keeping a close eye on Stacy who was now committed to life in California and equally committed to finding ways to deliver misery to my life.

I looked at my ring and smiled to myself while hugging Manuel.

Bring it, bitch.

PUSHED TIMES, CHEWING PEPPER

PART ONE

MYRA JOLIVET

A SARAH DOUCETTE JEAN-LOUIS MYSTERY

Pushed Times, Chewing Pepper

Sarah Doucette Jean-Louis is a rare woman. She is marked for murder while a suspected accessory to the mysterious murder plot. She is a trained family therapist who has a difficult time tolerating her own family for more than lunch. She is a contemporary California native with old world, Louisiana Creole roots. Her aunts and grandparents regularly talked to the dead and cast spells. They thought everyone did.

In one year, Sarah's life is a haze of martini hangovers, a stalker, the wrong man, fights with a bitch cousin and the voodoo wisdom of her Aunt Cat. Then comes Michael . . . and it gets worse. Deception and disappointment bring Sarah the hardest times she's ever known and propel her into a new life. The Creoles say, "Pushed times will make a monkey chew pepper." It means that challenging times inspire unique actions. Sarah learns to use her psychic gifts for guidance and to open her mind to unique actions. Her worst year becomes the best life-changing time of her life.

Get the first book in the Sarah Doucette Jean-Louis mystery series on Amazon.

49254098R00095

Made in the USA
San Bernardino, CA
21 August 2019